Who's Going To Pray For Me Now?

Niles Reddick

ISBN: 978-1-945917-86-8

Printed in the United States of America

Cover design: Tracey Ranauro
Cover art: *Who, if I cried out, would hear me among the Angelic Orders?* from Rainer Maria Rilke, photo by T.D. Liskey

Also by Niles Reddick:
Drifting too far from the Shore
If Not for You
Reading the Coffee Grounds
Road Kill Art and Other Oddities
Lead Me Home

"Making other books jealous since 2004"

Big Table Publishing Company
San Francisco, CA
www.bigtablepublishing.com

Acknowledgments

"Who's Going To Pray For Me Now?" *Anti-Heroin Chic*, first publication; *Yellow Mama*, second publication
"Flash in the Pan" *Vestal Review*
"Come for Me" *Litro*
"Chill" *The Wild Word*
"Torpor" *South Shore Review*
"Collectibles" *Marriage Lifespan*
"Allergic" *Midway Journal*
"Precognition" *Bosphorus Review of Books*
"Bust of Zeb" *Fiction Kitchen*
"Madame Tussaud's" *Danse Macabre*
"Thunderbird" *Ego Phobia*
"Going to the Movie with Elvis" *3rd Wednesday*
"Crying Boy" *The Wild Word*
"A Drunk Cedar Waxwing" *London Independent Story Prize Anthology*
"Segway" *Abergavenny Press*
"Paradise Cove" *Stereo Stories*
"Snowplow Driver" *I-70 Review*
"Hospitality" *The Museum of Americana*
"Turret" *Borderless Journal*
"Alien" *The Wild Word*
"Ten Commandments" *WINK*
"The Rejection" *WINK*
"Smoking in a Storm" *The Hong Kong Review*
"Elevator Ride" *Blaze Vox*
"A Writer's Trophies" *PIF*
"Keys" *The Journal of Compressed Creative Arts*
"Jim Moore Restoration" *Believeau Press*
"Rodeo Drive" *New Reader Magazine*
"Taking up Serpents" *Yorick Radio Productions*
"Gobekli Tepe" *Fiction Menteur/Paris Lit Up*
"Licking the Beaters" *MacQueen's Quinterly*
"Yellow Wood" *Dead Fern Press*

"Point Dume" *New Feather Anthology*
"Intuition" *Instant Noodles*
"Bitten" *Spelt: Celebrating the Rural Experience*
"Gently Used Boat, Motor, and Trailer" *The Rye Whiskey Review*
"The Scream" *Feisty Runts*
"Mandela Effect" *Roi Faineant Literary Press*
"Agitator" *Fleas on the Dog Press*
"Garden Party" *The Muleskinner Journal*
"Thirst" *Valiant Scribe*
"Little Dom's" *Academy of the Heart and Mind*
"Engagement Ring" *Sage Cigarettes*
"Box of Polaroids" *Lunate*
"How to Spend Christmas Alone at Motel 6" *Danse Macabre*
"No Bail" *Nunum*
"Back in My Day" *Right Hand Pointing*
"Roch", "Dads" and "Flatfooted Fred" *The Dribble Drabble Review*
"Polo Shirts" and "Panhandler" *Terror House*
"A Piece of Pencil Lead" *The Red Lemon Review*
"Needle Teeth" *Linea*
"Three-Day Holiday Weekend" *Fairfield Scribes*
"Vampire" and "Our Baby" *Five Minute Lit.*

Table of Contents

For Raymond and Beverly, Bobbie, and Nan

"Who, if I cried out, would hear me
among the Angelic Orders?"
~ Rainer Maria Rilke

Who's Going to Pray for Me Now?

The deputy who called shared that you'd gone to the restroom to pee, that your jeans had fallen to your knees, that your arm and hand were outstretched and propped on the wall, a brace that didn't hold unlike the spec homes you'd built for Habitat after hurricanes along the Gulf. They said you couldn't go because your kidneys had stopped functioning and filtering, and within a short time, your heart stopped, and you were gone. I wondered if that was what death was like—an incredible urge to pee and the sweet relief of finally going. I imagined you flew through that sheetrock and roof, looked back down on yourself all humped over with muscle turned to flab and your body looked like a cicada shell stuck on the limb of a tree. After I wiped tears, the first thing that came to mind was who was going to pray for me now that you're gone.

I remember that long ride to see you in Texas in Daddy's Ford LTD with the pop-up headlights and fender skirts I thought were so cool and didn't understand why car companies stopped making them, or the white wall tires that were hard to keep white. Daddy made me put white shoe polish on them when we couldn't get oil stains off. I remember Nana trying to act like riding in the back seat didn't bother her, and since she never drove and never trusted Daddy and certainly didn't trust him after that car was passing others on our side and was headed straight for us, how she kept punching her floorboard with her foot from the backseat to stop, and how Daddy'd said, "If they want to play chicken, I'll show them who the king of the road is." Daddy sped up until he side-swiped them, and we landed in a shallow bayou, an alligator swimming close to the front of the car, and Nana out cold because the iron skillet she had to bring because "I ain't gonna scramble no eggs in a new-fangled pan Joe bought from the Sears and Roebuck catalogue." At first, we thought she was dead until we saw the iron skillet had slid off the back-deck window and landed on her head.

We only stayed a few days because y'all fought when drinking hard liquor, you a Chevy man and Daddy a Ford man who got mad when you said Ford stood for "fix or repair daily," and the ride home was miserable because we were crammed in that Japanese compact, but it was the only rental Daddy could afford because his insurance didn't cover rentals. You and Daddy didn't talk much, and you didn't come visit even when Nana died from that brain aneurysm, and you called and said you couldn't believe she was gone, that she was stubborn, Daddy was just like her, and it was her own fault because of that damned skillet she brought to Texas that had knocked her out and later paved the way for her aneurysm. You thought it was ironic that Nana died quickly and at home since she never got in another vehicle after she got back from Texas, walked to the grocery store and to appointments, and certainly wouldn't have gone to the hospital in an ambulance.

I am happy you quit drinking, got saved, and prayed for me every day. Sometimes, I could feel those prayers like a gentle breeze giving me comfort from the blistering heat, the same way you described a breeze when you could still put asphalt shingles on a roof before you slipped, fell, broke your back and had to take disability. I was happy you prayed for Daddy, and even though he only drinks Schlitz at night when he curses and damns everyone in Washington to hell, he still drinks Crown on the weekends and eats his eggs from Nana's skillet with the big spoon because he can't hold them on a fork since he has tremors. I'm praying for him like you prayed for me, but it doesn't seem to take hold, and I'm hoping you find Nana and come for him when he takes his last sip, which may be soon because if he curses me one more time while I'm over here on the sofa minding my own business, I may take that skillet to his head.

Flash in the Pan

My first wife Kat rolled the dough in balls, flattened them, cut a hole in the center, and slid them in the hot grease, which created a flash in the pan—rolling smoke, popping grease, and bubbling that lasted until the dough reached a high temperature and turned brown. She then pulled them out with tongs, put them on paper towels to soak up the grease, and dried them before pouring a lemon and sugar mixture icing on top. Nothing beat her homemade donuts, not even a brain-freezing strawberry daiquiri on a blazing hot day at the beach.

As an engineer, I saw life in an unemotional, mechanical way with an occasional flash in the pan. Kat, on the other hand, saw life as mostly ordinary, except for emotional bursts of feeling on her timeline: giving birth to our only son, birthday cake, occasional wine and sex, opening presents Christmas morning, salvation or baptism, and even death when one journeyed the tunnel to the light.

When she journeyed after that train hit her Camry, at first, I thought about her a lot. I wondered why her and not someone else. I wondered if she'd suffered. I wondered how I'd get by without her. I knew I'd never eat another donut like hers. Then, I thought about her on special occasions--birthdays, anniversaries, and Christmas. Once I was in Wal-Mart, smelled her Chanel #5 perfume, and turned to look down the toilet paper aisle to see if she was there.

I saw her one night when I dreamed I died. It seemed less mechanical, more fluid. I was in the pine box on display for others, looked at myself, and thought I looked better dead than alive. The smile creases around my mouth were gone, the stress and worry wrinkles on my forehead from scrunching eyebrows had dissipated, and the crow's feet around my eyes had smoothed. Whether death had relaxed my skin or whether the embalming fluid had filled me until smooth, I didn't know, but the suit and tie I'd worn once to Kat's funeral still looked good on me and my hair looked better smoothed down with gel.

I hugged people who were there, some dead and some living, mostly cousins and friends from school I hadn't seen for fifty years. I never thought it was odd I was both dead and alive. Kat was there, sitting in the first pew, and whispered to me, "I told you it wasn't just a flash in the pan. Feel your life." I woke up, my pillow wet. I craved her donuts, called our son who works in IT, has his own family, and lives on the West coast, and decided to stop by Wal-Mart and ask the widowed cashier out for dinner.

Back in My Day

Dad brought home an empty cardboard box from work and put it on the living room floor.

"Why did you bring that home?" Mom asked.

"For the kids," Dad said.

"You don't know where it's been."

We didn't care where it had been, as the three of us piled in and sat in a row for a bumpy bus ride across town to Sears' candy counter, then piloted a swooping jet to drop bombs in the jungles of Viet Nam until we were shot down like our uncle Ray, and then drove a dune buggy to the beach and zig-zagged the wet sand to avoid the washed-up jellyfish, seaweed, and broken shells.

"I'm throwing that out tomorrow," Mom said, but we knew she didn't mean it.

Come for Me

The sweat from the heat and humidity made our skin stick to the vinyl seats of the 1965 Skylark, and with windows rolled down to keep us cool, gnats blew in and collided with our eyes or tongues if our mouths were open. On the thirty-minute drive to our grandmother's clapboard house off the ground and resting on old brick pylons every Sunday after church, we often napped, being lullabied to sleep by the rhythmic ticking of the Skylark like a sewing machine, and then, waking up with seat creases on our cheeks that grandmother kissed when she hugged us and offered us pound cake and sweet tea.

We swung in the wooden swing, creaking back and forth, or rocked in paint-pealing chairs while she and my parents talked of weather, war, politics, or relatives. Sometimes, we shelled peas, snapped green beans for her in metal bowls, or shucked corn, and she canned or froze our labors for reunions or funerals, where people would bless and compliment her.

We hated going every week and whined, but our mother said, "We come for her because she'd come for you." We would much prefer our friends' trampoline across the street, the coolness of the community pool, or riding bicycles on the railroad tracks until the whistle blasted and warned us off, but at our grandmother's, we explored the shed out back with antique green glass bottles and jars or searched for treasure while crawling under the house on the cold dirt avoiding elaborate spider webs, big cockroaches, or even an occasional rat snake.

When it was time to leave before dark, our mother's hands would dust us off, tell us we were filthy, and that she might not be able to get the stains out of our clothes. When we were home, she directed us to take a bath in the claw feet tub with soap our grandmother had made and gifted us at Christmas, a gift that disappointed us even though our parents had told us in advance to be appreciative, say thank you, because we didn't want to hurt her feelings. She didn't have money for dolls, trains, or sports equipment.

When her heart sputtered and stopped in her chest, she simply left us one hot and humid summer day, like that Skylark that stopped running after fifteen years. Now over fifty years later, I long for those sticky seats on Sunday and visits at my grandmother's house. With her genetic make-up and my own heart skipping beats, I'm hopeful that she'll come for me, and we can rock on a porch and talk about weather, war, politics, and relatives.

Box of Polaroids

When my grandmother was in the kitchen, I opened the box that had its permanent home under her coffee table, and the black wrought iron oscillating fan cooled the sweat from anxiety as I pulled out the Polaroids of the grandfather I never knew. Donned in a black tie and suit with his thin-lipped smile, he was posed for last photos, eyes closed with a thin layer of makeup for color. The next photo showed the casket right where the coffee table was near the fireplace, flower funeral sprays flanking each end of the silver casket.

Family photos of deceased great aunts, uncles, cousins on my grandmother's front porch revealed dreamier, younger, and thinner times when everyone smoked, dipped, or chewed tobacco, and I wished they, their children, or grandchildren had kept and stored the classic cars parked willy-nilly in the yard, careful though not to crush my grandmother's daylily beds surrounded by rock, carefully weeded, and arranged by variety and color. A convertible Mustang, a Land Rover Defender, and Karmann Ghia would have made for a great collection of classics that could have been restored and converted to electric and worth more than they ever would have dreamed when they purchased them new, but I supposed they were in Frank's junk yard, a cemetery for cars just down the highway after their valves went bad, transmissions failed, or their systems just blew out in one final ride and were hauled to Frank's by the ambulance of a tow truck to harvest and salvage parts to keep others running smoothly, unlike my grandfather, who could not be saved back then.

When I heard my grandmother's pumps tick-tocking across the wooden floor, I closed the box of polaroids and put it back before she caught me and became sad again.

Chill

Sam invited Will and Jack over to hang out and chill, since it was a holiday weekend. They used to call it a spend the night or sleepover, but now, that seemed childish. Sam's dad Bobby agreed to grill burgers, and Sam's mom Sheila picked up two-liter sodas and chips at the grocery store. Sheila knew the three teens would stay upstairs, watching movies or playing games on the X-box. She also knew they would stay up past midnight, likely until 3:00 a.m., but with the air purifier running, Sheila hoped she wouldn't hear them.

Jack bounced in the door, his moppy hair flopping, but there was something strange about Will. His head was down, and he was less communicative than Sheila recalled. With teens, their bad moods could be from a pimple, a bad grade, or being ignored by a girl. When the boys went upstairs, Sheila cleaned the table and noticed Will hadn't eaten.

Bobby went to bed early, and Sheila read a magazine with television news playing in the background. She heard updates about the Russian war in the Ukraine, the shift from early spring weather back to cold, and something local about a bad wreck with a fatality.

Sam came downstairs and said, "Mom, did Will come down here?"

"No, I don't think so."

"I think he left." Sam went to the window. "His car's not here."

"He didn't seem like himself. He didn't touch his food. Something wrong?"

"I don't think so." Sam went back upstairs.

Sheila decided to text Will's mom and ask her if everything was alright. It took a while before his mother responded, "He didn't make it."

Sheila didn't understand until she got other texts and calls that Will had been killed in a head-on collision. She cried and felt she should have stopped him from leaving their house. They all went to Will's funeral days later, and Sam seemed very depressed.

After a few weeks, Sheila saw Will's mom at the grocery store, they hugged, and Sheila confessed her guilt at not stopping Will from leaving their house. Will's mom told Sheila, "He was on his way to your house when he had the wreck. He never made it to your house." Sheila didn't contradict her because of her grief, and Sheila told Bobby when he got home.

"That's weird."

"You think he was killed and still came here?"

"That's absurd."

Sheila googled and read the news accounts on her iPad. She knew what time they had eaten, because of the local news, and she recalled his wreck being on the news. She remembered his head being down, his not eating, his disappearance, and his car not being in the driveway. She speculated at the end of life, especially if it's a sudden and tragic death, that one might continue the same path until the energy fades. The truth gave her a sudden chill and goosebumps, but she decided not to tell Sam or Bobby until later.

No Bail

His mother wouldn't put up bail money. "Let him sit in there, sober up, and think about his life," she said.

Tom spent three days in jail before the police department released him. He'd have to report to court in thirty days to address the driving under the influence charges, but he maintained his innocence. He said he wasn't driving because he'd fallen asleep in the Taco Bell drive-thru. No doubt he was UI, but not DUI.

Sadly, Tom lost his job at the plant for not calling in because he'd wasted his one call on his mother.

Torpor

The snow fell for two days straight and added inches on top of what was already thick layers from two months of winter weather. Edna hadn't walked to the mailbox by the road for a week for fear of falling. Last month, she'd fallen and landed on ice on the back stoop, hurting her knee, when she threw out the last of the birdseed. It took a couple of weeks before she stopped limping.

Edna didn't care about the mail. She knew what bills came when, and she knew it was mostly junk—statements from her insurance company about medication, political fliers, and travel magazines about cruise ships sailing to the Caribbean and South America. She knew that's where the swallows, martins, and warblers had gone, flying thousands of miles because of their internal clocks, but she wouldn't see them because she couldn't afford a cruise.

Yesterday, Edna put on her heavy coat, gloves, and a hat and looked out the window, but she couldn't see her flower beds with hostas and variegated liriope. When she opened the garage, she knew her Thunderbird would back over a small mound of snow that had blown against the garage door. She'd called ahead and ordered grocery items and didn't plan to brave the grocery store parking lot because it wasn't cleared. One of the clerks brought what little she ordered and placed the bags on the floorboard of the Thunderbird's backseat, including the bird seed.

When the temperature rose and the sun was out, birds came out of torpor to hunt for worms, insects, berries, seeds, and resembled colorful polka dots on the white landscape. In torpor, their body's metabolism slowed by ninety-five percent, their body temperature lowered, and energy was conserved until weather conditions improved, sometimes after a few hours or overnight. The birds didn't burn as much body fat and consumed less oxygen.

If Edna didn't drink coffee when she woke up, she felt like she was in torpor. After a light breakfast, Edna opened the back door and tossed a cup of bird seed into the yard. She then reclined her chair and half-watched a program about bird migration, covered up with a blanket, and closed her eyes. She discovered herself flying with the swallows, martins, and warblers. The views were incredible, and the sounds of the different types of birds together in the sky were symphonic.

Her daughter found her in the recliner after she hadn't answered repeated calls, paramedics transported Edna to the hospital, and emergency room personnel thought she had heart failure. Her heart rate had slowed, her body temperature had decreased, but Edna wasn't in torpor. She enjoyed the mountain forests, the cool waterfalls, the warm temperatures, and the bird symphony in South America, and she planned to stay.

Collectibles

Magnolia Park is located in the older part of Burbank and is also where many of the hipper antique stores, independent coffee shops, and fantastic bookstores can be found. Manning had been in the collectible business since he and his wife moved to Burbank in the 1950s. Marie had started as a secretary at Warner Brothers, but before she retired after thirty years, her title had become administrative assistant. Her job duties hadn't changed, but she had never complained and had loved her career at Warner Brothers. She'd told Manning, "It's the symbol that survives, like the WB one on the water tower."

Manning had responded, "You're always right." He'd brushed her cheek with his fingers, and when she died of a massive stroke, he brushed her check and said, "I'll miss you, Marie."

It had been Marie's idea for him to open the shop, and he named it after her: Marie's Collectibles. Through the years, he'd scooped up some nice antique pieces in Burbank, pieces he located at early morning garage sales. If the garage sale was at an actor's house, that was an automatic mark-up. He'd collected and sold a wooden ironing board from Doris Day, a broach from Jane Wyman (President Reagan's first wife), a signed copy of *To Kill a Mockingbird* to Robert Redford, and some weights from Denzell Washington.

In addition, Marie brought home anything discarded at WB, and if there was a story associated with it, that was pure profit, profit to put their daughter through UCLA, pay cash for her first car, cover her wedding expenses, and help them with a down payment on her first house, a bungalow near the Frank Lloyd Wright homes and Griffith Observatory that overlooked Los Angeles.

Collectibles Marie rescued from the dumpster were an ashtray Betty Davis used in her dressing room that Manning had sold for twenty dollars; a hairbrush used by Joan Crawford that brought fifty dollars; a broken watch left behind by Douglas Fairbanks fetched two hundred dollars; and a broken cap gun used by John Wayne that brought nearly five hundred dollars.

If Marie and Manning became aware of a major change in society, like the development of cellular phones, they scooped up items like rotary phones or phone books. They even found several Burbank phone books with Johnny Carson's photo on the cover, and those items brought high dollar. When there was a lull in business, Manning expanded. He added an online store in eBay, which increased his sales to worldwide audiences who might never visit the Burbank store. Success followed, and he and Marie had talked of retirement, moving into the Santa Monica mountains.

When Manning arrived at Marie's Collectibles a few weeks after Marie had died, there was a rare rain coming down, and he stood under the checkered owning, opened the door lock, heard the bell jingle, and smelled Marie's perfume. It wasn't overwhelming, but just a brief whiff, and he heard her words, "It's the symbol that survives." It was as though Marie whispered it in his ear.

Manning knew it was truth. The actor doesn't survive. While the film or television show technically survives, it isn't constantly shown. The times don't survive. The one thing that survives is the symbol, like the WB symbol on the iconic water tower. Recently, in a video tour, Ellen DeGeneres welcomed visitors from the small balcony that circled the tower, but Manning's friend Ralph who was a retired teacher and had taken a job as a tour guide told him: "They filmed her in the studio and projected the image of her onto that balcony. It would be way too dangerous to hoist her up there." It made sense to Manning.

Warner Brothers had sets that were used over and over like the New York Street set complete with an overhead subway track. From *Yankee Doodle Dandy* in 1942 to *Wonder Woman* in 1975 to *Friends* in 1994, the New York Street set had survived. The Jungle Lagoon was another example of a set that first appeared in the 1956 feature film *Santiago*, later in the 1993 Spielberg film *Jurassic Park*, and again in the 2018 film *Aquaman*. The Midwestern town square with a gazebo was used in feature films from the 1960's such as *The Music Man* and

Bonnie and Clyde to television series like *The Dukes of Hazard*, *Gilmore Girls*, and *Pretty Little Liars*. Viewers were not aware that these sets appeared in multiple films or television series that spanned decades or that they might be rented to other studios who were scouting for sets.

Marie's whisper prompted Manning to pick up the phone and call his friend Ralph.

"Funny thing you should call," Ralph said. "I was just thinking about you. They've tossed these signs from the New York, Lagoon, and Midwestern sets in the dumpster that have been used for years. Making some new ones. You want me to get them for you?"

"Absolutely," Manning said. "Signs bring a great price." Manning knew he would get top dollar for them. He added, "Glad you are on the inside of the studio fence. Since Marie's gone, I need someone to get me some treasures, so I can supplement my Medicare."

"Supplementing Medicare is the main reason I came back to work. That and to see if I can get discovered and be an extra in a film."

"They've already made *Cocoon* and *The Golden Girls*. It would have to be a new film or show with seniors."

Ralph laughed. "Yeah, you're probably right. I'll drop the signs off later this afternoon."

"I appreciate it and I'll split the profit with you."

"Sounds great."

Manning hung up the phone and knew Marie had steered him in the right direction. Their love and marriage bond seemed to survive death. He'd see to it these new collectibles, too, would survive long after he and his friend Ralph were gone.

Allergic

The whole family was allergic. Bill was allergic to penicillin and had ballooned up and changed colors after he'd had a shot for a sinus infection. He looked like Violet on *Willie Wonka and the Chocolate Factory* who'd swelled from chewing gum. Fortunately, the clinic's nurse had given him a shot with an EpiPen. Bill's wife Sara was allergic to ants and had stood in a bed of ants while fishing as a child and had to be given multiple Benadryls. She was adamant that they had a bag of ant killer every spring just in case. The first sign of a dirt mound and ants were sent scrambling to neighbors' yards by the poison granules. Their daughter Ann was allergic to wasps, and when early signs of spring such as buds on dogwood trees and new sprigs of grass, Bill was sure to get the can of jet stream wasp spray to kill any eggs in nests. Their son Kyle was "allergic" to onions, liver, and anything else he didn't want to eat that his mom cooked, and he was great at embellishing symptoms, real or imagined. His mom suspected an incarnation of the boy who cried wolf, but she didn't share with Bill and simply pampered Kyle in hopes he'd grow out of it.

"I believe I'm developing a new allergy," Sara said while tossing the decorative throw pillows into the chair in the bedroom, fluffing their pillows, and pulling back the comforter.

"To what?" Bill asked.

"Mom," she said.

"Don't be silly," he said. "You're half her, so you can't be allergic."

"But when I talk to her, I begin to itch, clear my throat, and get hot flashes."

"Maybe you're going through the change."

"Now, *you* don't be silly. I've had a hysterectomy."

"Well, maybe you are allergic, then. Hell, I don't know. I've got to get up early." Bill pulled back the sheet, eased into the bed, made noises, and closed his eyes.

"Maybe it's because her health is declining, and she tells me things that I don't really want to hear. The other day, she called and told me she'd lived through gall bladder, hemorrhoid, and carotid artery surgeries and didn't want to have cataract surgery. Said one of her friends told her they take out your eyeball and she's worried they might drop it. I tried to tell her they don't take out the eye, but she didn't believe me."

"She ought to be worried about her mind if she believes that nonsense."

"Well, she's worried about her mind, too, since we've talked about taking her car. Says she doesn't know how she'll get to the library to get her books. All she does is read Harlequin romance novels all day, sometimes two and three a day."

"They're all the same. Fantasies. No relationship works like a Harlequin one."

"She told me the other day she enjoys her imaginary lovers more than she enjoyed dad when he was here."

"Now, that's just wrong. I don't want to hear about that. She better not let that get back to the women's group at the Methodist church or they'll boot her out."

"She told me she can't remember which books she's read, so now, she's marking every page sixty-five with a pencil, so she can pull them and see if she's read them before she checks them out."

"That old librarian will have her put in jail for marking all those books!"

"She called me today and read me her obituary."

"What? Does she think she's getting ready to check out?"

"Said she didn't want us to worry about having to write it, but when I suggested some different wording, she told me not to correct her, that she was still my mother, and I wasn't too old for some punishment."

"Sounds like she may be losing it if she thinks she can come over and whip you."

"I know. Maybe I'm not allergic. Maybe it's just anxiety."

"Well, go get you some of those melatonin gummies in the pantry and take a handful, so you can sleep."

"Okay. Maybe tomorrow will be better. Maybe I'll take her on a picnic."

"Great idea," said Bill and turned on his side.

The hair on his back and his misshapen abdomen spread made Sara think he was a gigantic grotesque fly like Jeff Goldblum had played in the movie. She suddenly felt allergic to Bill and went to the kitchen for melatonin. She planned to take her mother to the library after the picnic and decided she'd get a Harlequin just for fun.

Three-Day Holiday Weekend

Leck saw broken glass shattered on asphalt, spent fireworks in yards, trees, shrubbery, and on roofs, and beer and soft drink cans along the curbs. He noticed a lone shoe, a smushed squirrel, and a hair weave in the road. A stop sign had been hit and bent like a palm tree in a hurricane. He knew cats and dogs suffered from post-traumatic stress disorder and cowered under beds while their owners had gas, their arteries pumped cholesterol, uric acid caused swelling for gout flares, and headaches pounded from beer consumed on the three-day holiday weekend.

Precognition

He craved a grilled cheese, took the old frying pan, put it on the stove's eye, and dabbed enough butter to coat the pan. He peeled the American cheese from its wrapper, put it between two slices of wheat bread, and placed it in the pan. When he turned to get the spatula out of the utensil drawer, he saw a flash of the momentary future in his mind's eye: the stove's burner exploding, the pan and bits of grilled cheese flying across the small kitchen in the garage apartment, bits of sandwich on the floor, roof, cabinets, and him cleaning up and scraping bits of cheese before the mice came out at night and nibbled. He wondered if he had to buy a new burner, install it on the stove, or if the landlord would repair it. He listened to his rumbling, hungry stomach still craving a hot grilled cheese.

Once he grabbed the spatula, and before he turned back to flip his grilled cheese, he heard the pop, like a firecracker, and watched in slow motion as the chaotic scene he'd just seen in his mind's eye unfolded before him. He hadn't thought it would happen. His precognition didn't always work.

He knew if he had been standing in front of the stove when the burner exploded that he might have had bits of the burner in his eyes or face and was appreciative of the precognitive moment, a gift he'd had since childhood when he had been zapped by an electrical outlet in a storm as he tried to plug in his electric train set in his bedroom. His hair on his legs, arms, and head had stood at attention, better than his toy soldiers, and when Seth brushed his hair, it returned to its standing position. It took a day before it laid down again.

Later, he learned that he had to be careful around electricity, as if the electricity itself was attracted to him. He had been jolted by an electric fence while brushing his horse Pinto, and when he swung in a tire swing in the live oak tree in their backyard, lightning split the tree in two, and he felt it throughout his body. After that incident, anytime he wore a watch, the watch stopped completely. He'd come to rely on others for time.

Seth didn't consider his experience paranormal; he simply believed it was part of the everyday reality anyone could experience if the conditions were right. He had simply acquired something that aided him in self-preservation, like a guardian angel guiding him, but Seth didn't share it outside his circle of friends or family. Seth adjusted to the precognition like it was a part of him like an extra finger, webbed toes, or a limp in his gait. He cleaned up pieces of the broken pan and bits of grilled cheese, tossed them in the trash, and made himself a cold cheese sandwich.

Bust of Zeb

Mark was recovering and staying in a halfway house just two blocks from downtown, and each day, he put on a clean t-shirt, his jeans, and his sandals and walked downtown to work at a café in exchange for free meals and minimum wage. Each day, he walked through a newly built park next to a roundabout, and he thought he heard whispering.

"Help me. Why am I here?"

Mark knew withdrawals had strange effects, but he felt he had passed those and wondered if it was the wind, a bird, or squirrel that made the sound. He even wondered if perhaps his hearing had been damaged from all the alcohol and drugs.

* * *

A few months before, the mayor had finally convinced the City Council to vote on the roundabout because other progressive cities had one and more importantly, he agreed he would personally pay for a small park with a bust of Zeb, an old merchant who was what the mayor called a king maker. Zeb had put most of them in office with his financial support and influence and had been rumored to help three governors, one of whom had gone on to the U.S. Senate and then served under Clinton. Zeb had recently been killed in a head on collision with a beer truck. He'd been eighty-five and had weaved over the line as he was reaching in his pocket to get his glasses.

The mayor and others had a nice dedication, but the bronze bust looked like a ritualistic shrunken head from the Amazon jungles of Peru. Tribes believed shrunken heads held the souls of the deceased and wouldn't harm them.

One of the council members commented, "Mayor, if you couldn't afford a realistic bust, then we could have come up with the difference."

"Well, Zeb's head always seemed a bit small to me," he responded.

"But he had big ideas," the councilman responded, and they all chuckled.

* * *

On his way back to the halfway house, Mark sat on the bench next to the pedestal where Zeb's bust rested. He opened the brown paper bag and bit into his turkey reuben sandwich.

"Get me out of here."

Mark looked around. He recalled hearing the earlier whisper. He decided to try something. "Is someone whispering to me?"

"Yes. You can hear me?"

"I believe so."

"Can you get me out of here? If you can't, can you at least get this bird shit out of my eyes and off my nose?"

Mark turned toward the bust of Zeb. He put his sandwich back in the bag and took his napkin, spit on it, and rubbed the shit off the bust. "Is that better?"

"Yes, thank you. Can you go to the mayor's office and tell him I'm in here? I'm an old friend of his. I'm a bit pissed that he made me a shrunken head out of bronze. Everyone laughs at me when they drive by. I knew I shouldn't have supported him. Even the birds have turned me into some sort of shit target."

Mark said, "Well, I can't do that today, maybe tomorrow if I have time."

The next day, Mark walked a different direction to the café downtown, but walked past Zeb on the way back to the halfway house. "Hey, did you see him?"

"Not today, but maybe tomorrow," Mark responded.

"Supposed to get cold. Can you bring me a knit cap to put on my head?"

"I'll see what I can do."

On the third day, Mark put a knit cap on Zeb's head. "Hope this will keep you warm."

"Thank you so much. Will you see the mayor today?"

"You know, Zeb, I think they'll put me back in detox or increase my meds if I go see the mayor and tell him a shrunken head statue is giving me messages unless you can give me some sort of specifics."

"Tell you what. You got any money?"

"Dude, I'm not giving a shrunken head statue any money."

"No, listen. Tonight is the lottery. Use these numbers and get one ticket. Don't be greedy. You can only win once. Write them down."

Mark took a pen from his pocket, jotted the numbers on his paper bag with his supper inside, and thanked Zeb. He stopped in the convenience store, bought one ticket, and that night when the numbers were announced, he learned he'd won 1.5 million dollars. He took an uber to the lottery office, showed his ticket, and they wrote him a check, minus taxes. He put the money in the bank and got a couple of blank cashier's checks and a platinum American Express. He bought a convertible Porsche, a condo on the lake, some furniture, and some new clothes. One day, he drove by the halfway house, cruised through the roundabout, and waved at Zeb. He wanted to thank him, but he thought it might be weird if someone saw him talking to a bust that looked like a shrunken head.

Madame Tussaud's

I didn't know that one of the first wax models Madame Tussaud made was when the famous French writer Voltaire modeled for her. She taught votive making to King Louis XVI's sister Elizabeth and lived at Versailles for years. The brochure read that her legend lived on in museums across the globe, but we didn't want to spend nearly one hundred fifty dollars to see wax figures of famous people and characters conjured by Hollywood. When we couldn't score free tickets to *The Ellen DeGeneres Show* or *Jimmy Kimmel Live*, we decided to splurge and visit the wax museum anyway because of our son who pleaded he could get pictures with Aquaman, Spiderman, and Superman, heroes to him from cartoons, films, and X-box games.

Making our way down the star Walk of Fame, we had to step over a homeless woman sleeping next to the star of Lois Lane from *Superman.* We also had to fend off tour salesmen, a woman who would create a star in the sidewalk for tourists, and people dressed like Freddy Krueger, Batman, and even Mickey Mouse. We also had to shoo "I Ride Like a Star" Ferrari tour up Mulholland Drive salesmen and vendors selling food and drinks. We felt like fish swimming upstream, but the fading sun and lights from Griffith Observatory shown bright on the infamous Hollywood hillside sign but were no match for the lights on Hollywood's star walk. We bought our tickets, masked up, and were encouraged to take plenty of photos.

We were exhausted from walking miles from our hotel to see various tourist attractions, to eat at famous restaurants like In and Out and Fat Sal's, and from jet lag from losing three hours from Eastern Time to Pacific Time, so we blinked several times to make certain the wax figures were indeed wax. They seemed even more real than the real people seemed on TV whether it was historical figures who were no longer living such as Audrey Hepburn from *Breakfast at Tiffany's*, Patrick Swayze from *Dirty Dancing,* or Clark Gable from *Gone with the Wind.* Clothing, hair, expressions, and even eyes seemed perfect, as if they had been simply stopped and were preserved in time.

There were moments when I felt like the wax figures might be watching us, as if their eyes followed us around the room, and several times, I walked back just to doublecheck. I took photos with Tom Hanks as Forrest Gump on the park bench with his box of chocolates on his lap, Patrick Stewart who played Jean Luc Picard on *Star Trek the Next Generation* from the Captain's chair on the bridge of the U.S.S. Enterprise, and even with ET in a basket on the bicycle, and my photos seemed as real as the shows and films I had watched. Suddenly, I'd gone from the sidelines of our living room to front and center.

When we got to the second floor and found other wax stars, our amazement didn't fade, and as I stood next to the iconic Betty White, I heard a whisper, "Hey there." I know my eyes opened wide, and my wife said, "Come on, smile. Get closer to her. Maybe give her a kiss on the cheek."

"Yeah, baby. Give it to me." I turned and looked at her, and her eyes glistened.

"What are you doing?" my wife asked.

"I thought I heard something."

"Hurry up. I still want a pic of me with Marlon Brando. I always wanted to play Stella in the school play, but that slut Stephanie got the part. I want Jack Nicholson, too."

I turned back, smiled, and then, I felt someone pinch me on the ass. Betty had the same look on her face as if she'd done nothing and I turned around. There were no other tourists near the exhibit.

"Do you think there are actors playing the part of wax figures?"

"How many Xanax did you take for the cross country flight?"

"I only took four."

"How many were you supposed to take?"

"I could take up to two per day."

"Per day, right?"

"Well."

"No wonder you're so damned loopy. Come on."

As we walked out, I turned back, and Betty White winked at me. I smiled and blew her a kiss.

Thunderbird

I told them I was innocent, but the cops didn't believe me, my ex didn't believe me, and most of my friends and family didn't believe me either. I'd been in for five years, got my degree free online, and when I never expected it, one of the guards came to the door and said, "Man, it's your lucky day. You're out of here."

"What?"

"Yep, apparently you're innocent after all. So, you'll get a set of clothes, and the state will have to pay you back for your time. Startin' over money."

"Pay me back? Startin' over money? What the hell? I know I ought to forgive and forget, but I'm not going to, and I'll swear I'll sue somebody. I would have never killed my little girl. Do you know what happened to overturn the verdict?"

"You know they don't give us guards details, but the warden may know. He'll see you out."

When I met the warden, he told me they'd finally found my girl's remains in Denali's mountain forest not too far from the log cabin I'd rented for a vacation with sweet Claire. I could see it as clearly in my mind as if he happened yesterday. Claire was only five at the time and so petite. My ex Susan didn't want her to go with me. "What if something happens to you?" she'd said. I figured she was more concerned with me having some time with her after our divorce than she was worried about something happening to me. I was devastated when she disappeared. We'd been fishing at the lake, we had a fire going, and I walked into the woods just a few hundred yards to get more firewood, and when I walked back, she was gone. First, I thought she was playing a trick on me. She loved Hide and Seek. I called to her and looked around. Then, I worried she'd fallen in that lake. I called out and then dove in trying to see or feel for her. I came out of the lake, called the ranger's office miles away, and they said they would send assistance. It took thirty minutes before they got there, and we combed a radius around the lake and cabin, and there was no evidence at all. The sheriff's department even brought in the dogs, but it was like Claire was there one minute and gone the next. They couldn't pick up a scent from the blanket she slept with, her doll, or even a spare pair of shoes.

At night, I cried and prayed. I couldn't eat and lost twenty pounds in two weeks. The sheriff dredged the lake, but he was suspicious of me. He kept asking about the divorce, insinuating Claire liked her mother more, asked about my temper and bar room brawls I'd been in when I was young that he'd found on my record. The district attorney was itching to put me away.

"Warden, can you tell me anything else? What about Claire's remains?"

"They found them in a nest. A ranger spotted the bird, and he tracked it to a nest up the mountain near the top of a tree."

"Eagle or condor?"

"Nope. They believe it was a Thunderbird."

"What? I thought those were extinct or mythical. Part of Native lore."

"Well, so are giants and big foot, but you know, it's Alaska. Plenty of things hiding out there."

"I never would have guessed. I never saw it take her, didn't hear her scream, didn't see the bird at all, and never heard the noise of wings flapping."

"The ranger took some video with his phone. Son-of-a-bitch had a wingspan of twelve feet and took off as he approached. He found your girl's bones and a couple of other missing hikers. I'm sorry to be the one to tell you, but you can put this behind you now and move on. Start over with your life."

"Losing Claire was the worst thing that ever happened to me. I don't think you can put your child's death behind and move on. I wished that damned bird would've taken me, but the fact that no one ever believed me only added to my pain. I'm glad they found her remains and I'm glad I'm getting out." But he realized that he'd never truly be free.

Going to the Movie with Elvis

"Did I tell you about the time me and Elvis snuck out to see a movie?"

"Yes, you told me."

"We were in high school then, living at the Lauderdale Courts in Memphis. We went to see a late movie at the Loew's State Theatre on Second. We walked and Elvis wanted to listen to Sister Rosetta Tharpe on a replay of a gospel show on his transistor radio. I got in about two, but my parents thought I was asleep in my room. Mama got me up for school and said, 'You look like you didn't sleep well.' Then, the doorbell rang. I couldn't see who it was from the kitchen, but Mama uh-huh'd, came back in the kitchen, and said, 'That was Elvis. Said you left your coat on a bench outside and figured you might need it. You're grounded now for being out late.' 'But,' I said. 'No buts," she said. 'You need to quit hanging out with boys like Elvis. Thinks he's gonna be somebody.' 'He's just a guy who wants to be a singer,' I said. 'We all sing,' she snapped. Mama walked to the sink, washed the leftover grits from our bowls, and sat the bowls on a dish towel to dry. Mama didn't remember having said that when Elvis hit the big time with 'That's All Right.' You know, he was only 42 when he died. He'd be in his mid-80's like me if he were still around. Wish he was."

"Mr. Adams, you want some green or red Jell-O today?"

"I want some ice cream."

"The doctor won't let you have ice cream."

"Did I tell you about the time me and Elvis snuck out to see a movie?"

"You just rest a while, and I'll be back with your Jell-O."

Crying Boy

The boy looked like most. His brown hair had grown over his ears and fell below his brows. His red lips were full, but his eyes seemed larger and rounder than most. Tears came from both, ran down his face, and stopped before reaching his chin. The Spanish painter did an incredible job with the large teardrops. Different colors brushed onto the canvas, they looked identical to a large drop of water hanging on to a faucet and fighting gravity. Like the other thousands of originals and prints of *Crying Boy*, they were based on one street orphan in Barcelona, and the boy was painted with different backdrops, different outfits, and different poses.

My grandmother's *Crying Boy* was a print, not an original, and hung on the wall facing her wagon-wheel print sofa in the living room. Below the print was a gas space heater next to her Magnavox television encased in faux wood. There was a pine coffee table featuring wagon wheels on a hooked rug. I wasn't sure why she chose this print compared to the thousands of other possibilities, such as Dali, Van Gough, or Renoir; but they probably wouldn't have blended with her inexpensive early American motif. Depending on the selection, a Rockwell might have fit better.

When my grandmother climbed the wooden steps to her bedroom on the second floor of her Cape Cod just outside of Detroit, she undressed, got into bed, read for a bit, then fell asleep.

A fireman shattered her glass window from the ladder and yelled into her smoke-filled room, "Ms. Gaskins! Can you hear me?" She rolled out from her under her electric blanket, smelled the smoke, and saw the flashing lights from the firetruck reflecting on her neighbor's homes.

She coughed and yelled back, "Yes."

"Come on. I can't carry you. You'll need to jump. We'll catch you."

"I don't know about that," she told him.

She recounted to us almost every time we saw her that she knew she didn't think the life net would hold. She didn't know what was worse: burning to death in her house or her busting through the life net and breaking every bone in her body on the sidewalk below.

In an instant, she flung herself out the window and landed safely in the net. Though there were experiences in her lifetime that took longer and were more defining—giving birth to my mother that took twelve hours and her never letting my mother forget it, nursing her own mother through cancer and to the end of life tunnel, and having a wreck where something from the bottom of the car's dashboard punctured her appendix requiring life-saving, emergency surgery—the experience of flinging herself out of the window seemed to be the cherry on top of her ice cream sundae.

Sifting through the still warm ashes the next morning, she reached down and pulled a dirty *Crying Boy* from the debris. "Oh look!" She turned toward our family, held him up, and while he didn't look as young and innocent as he had hanging on her wall, he survived the fire with her. She put the print under her arm and vowed to hang him again.

My grandmother didn't know the history of the *Crying Boy* prints and paintings associated with fires and that the orphan who modeled for the painter grew up to burn to death in a car fire. The firemen investigators blamed discarded cigarettes, over-heated stoves, and faulty wiring of the hundreds of fires where the *Crying Boy* hung. My grandmother's fire was said to have started from the gas heater.

When she moved into the assisted living facility after her house burned, she told us, "You wouldn't believe how many people here have a different *Crying Boy* in their efficiency apartments." We never saw them but had no reason to doubt our grandmother. We recalled that information one morning when we got the call that a natural gas line exploded, leveling the assisted living facility and killing all the residents.

A Drunk Cedar Waxwing

The bird flew right into the front glass door, and we heard a thump. I figured it was neighborhood boys who'd thrown a ball at the house again. "By mistake," they'd squawked. The bird tried to move its wings but couldn't take flight. "What kind of bird is it?" I asked.

Robin said, "It's a Cedar Waxwing. Must be flying drunk." She opened the door, squatted, and took it gently in her hands.

"Drunk? I have heard of pilots flying drunk but not a bird."

"It's okay, pretty girl," she cooed. She stood and held the bird. "They eat fermented berries whole and often get drunk. Usually, they are in a flock, not alone."

I remember a chimney swift bird getting into Nana's house when I was a teen. It had been startled, and because the chimney flue was open, it flew inside instead of out. Nana shrieked as if it were a mouse in her pantry or a snake in her lilies, and while she limped and hid behind the door to the kitchen, she directed me to open the back door to the patio, to get the broom to scare and guide it outside without hitting it. The sooty gray bird flew out and within weeks, I could hear her babies screeching in the chimney.

With a few head shakes and flapping of its wings, the Cedar Waxwing took off, and I told Robin she should wash her hands.

Segway

My wife said she thought Segway meant moving from one topic to the next, and I told her that word was spelled "segue" but sounded the same and was similar in that a Segway took people from one place to the next. We'd never tried the two-wheeled scooters before, and to rent one was seventy-five dollars an hour per person for the four of us to follow a guide around downtown Greenville, South Carolina, a town in the foothills of the Appalachian Mountains. The experience was a natural one for my wife and teens, but I lagged; my legs stiffened and cramped almost immediately. Steering, too, was problematic, and I lurched forward almost hitting an elderly couple on the sidewalk.

The tour went through the West End of the city along Falls Park, but the best part to me was learning about the Greenville Spinners baseball history. From 1907 to 1962, the Greenville Spinners had been affiliated with major league teams including the Chicago White Sox, the Brooklyn Dodgers, and the Los Angeles Dodgers, but what impressed me most was that Shoeless Joe Jackson (who became known to non-baseball fans in the movie *Field of Dreams*) started with the Spinners in 1908 and was a native to the area. Tommy Lasorda had also played with them in 1949, but the list of known baseball alumni was long.

On the way back, we stopped on the Liberty Bridge that spanned the Reedy River in Falls Park downtown. The bridge was a curved, cantilevered, and cable work designed by Miguel Rosales, had won numerous design awards, and was unique to the United States. We gazed over the rails and listened to the water rushing over the boulders, and I wondered if the sounds were like what the Iroquois people must have experienced when they lived here by the river.

When the guide took off, my wife and teens followed closely behind, and I turned toward the bridge and slammed into the railing; the top half of my body lunged forward over the railing. My feet got caught up in the railing, or I would have splattered on the boulders in the river below.

My screams were enough to make the picnickers below on the banks of the Reedy wince while a couple of joggers came to my rescue, backed up the Segway, and helped me down to the bridge's deck. I looked ahead, and my wife and teens guffawed at my near-death experience while I muttered words not fit for anyone to hear.

I looked at the Segway, and a voice I recognized as my dad's from my distant past came barreling across time and directed me to "Get back on and try again" just like he had when he removed the training wheels from my bicycle, and I'd fallen off and into the ditch, scraped my arm, turned red in the face, and got frustrated. I nodded, took his fifty-year-old advice, and passed my family and the guide.

Vampire

She wore scrubs, touched my arm, told me to make a fist, tied it off with a rubber tube, swabbed a place with alcohol, inserted a needle, and filled three vials with blood. She didn't need fangs, and a cross wouldn't have kept her away, only an unpaid co-pay. With aid of equipment, the vampire would then gaze like Tiresias, the blind prophet of *Oedipus*, and make predictions from vitamin deficiency to high cholesterol to a high A1C. Knowing in advance what might come doesn't change the outcome, I'll be back for another bloodletting in six months.

Our Baby

While we thumbed magazine pages in the doctor's waiting area, we wondered if our baby would be alright, if there were additional vitamins or a prescription we might need, but when called back to the office, we were not prepared to hear, "We're sorry. There's no heartbeat." On the way home, the radio music didn't soothe, and I wondered why Hitler or Ted Bundy survived when our baby would not—what he or she might have been, an Einstein, or a Mother Teresa. We would never know, but we would try again.

Paradise Cove

We drove down the hill along a narrow road by the gated million-dollar trailer park at Malibu's Paradise Cove and breathed in one of the most beautiful scenes with the sea splashing against rocks below a cliff with small shrubs, cacti, and wildflowers. Neither of us had been here in over fifty years, and we were fortunate to make it to 2016 and have a fiftieth celebration. So many of our friends had divorced or slipped away early from disease, heart attacks, or strokes.

We had a seafood lunch, grilled salmon and shrimp, at the beach café, watched and listened to the waves crash near those sprawled on beach towels and in chairs to get sun, and we marveled at the rocks washed over millions of times to get their color and finish.

After lunch, we gathered our folding chairs, towels, umbrella, and carried our sandals, digging our toes in beach sand, where The Beach Boys were known for "Surfin' Safari" and Annette Funicello and Frankie Avalon starred in *Beach Blanket Bingo*. That's the first time I'd heard "He's My New Love" by Jackie Ward and The Hondells (lip-synched for the movie by Linda Evans who was in *The Big Valley* and *Dynasty*), and even though we'd lasted for over fifty years now, our old love still felt like new love. I had been an extra in a few films including *Beach Banket Bingo* in 1965 and hadn't been back to Paradise Cove since we'd been in Northern California our whole time together and rarely came back to Los Angeles since my parents had passed. I remember reading later that parts of *The Rockford Files* and *The Mod Squad* had been filmed here, too.

We cautiously climbed over rocks that jutted out and then curved back, creating a private barrier between us and the cove's sun bathers. We noted the mud slide signs, but we didn't think conditions were likely and stretched in our chairs under the umbrella. After watching waves crash onto the rocks, we heard the rushing, thundering mud slide: rocks, bushes, mud all rushing over the cliff.

We couldn't scramble quick enough and found we were covered in mud. I heard someone yell over the waves crashing to call 9 1 1, and several beach goers came to help and scooped mud. If there was a positive, it was that the umbrella had collapsed on our faces, and our airways were not clogged with mud, but I heard someone shout my husband wasn't breathing. I reached my hand toward his limp hand in the mud and touched it. "Come on," I whispered. "We still have some time. Our love can't be over yet."

One woman in a bikini came over, pushed both hands on his chest, pinched his nose, and breathed in and out for him. Within a couple of minutes, he coughed and vomited a bit into the mud. When emergency personnel arrived, they loaded us both onto stretchers, told us we would be okay, and carried us to the nearest hospital.

I later learned most of the mud and debris had gathered a few feet from us, covering rocks. We had experienced incredible beauty and disaster almost simultaneously. It also occurred to me that the beaches and coves were here when I was young and would be here long after we left, long after everyone in Malibu was gone. Nature always outlasts humanity. It was one constant that we knew. We were just appreciative for a little more time.

Snowplow Driver

When Josh and I left his grandmother's house in Rexburg, Idaho on highway 33 in his Pontiac Sunbird, there wasn't much scenery. Josh told me about the great flood in the area when the earthen Teton dam failed and that his relatives thought it was the end of the world. Josh wanted me to see giant paper mâché and cement Idaho potato on display on a flatbed trailer in Driggs, Idaho. I loved potatoes, but I didn't understand the tourism associated with a giant potato. I didn't want to hurt his feelings and snapped a photo. The sun was up, and the negative zero temperatures the previous night had risen to a whopping ten degrees. I didn't think I would want to live in a place so cold and wondered if residents simply adjusted or if they consumed something in their diet that helped them survive, like the Tibetan people's DNA had altered itself over time to accommodate the low oxygen levels at incredible heights.

Though everything was blanketed with snow, it hadn't snowed since we left the salt flats in Salt Lake City, Utah. "You think it'll snow?"

"Supposed to come in tonight, but we should be back from Jackson Hole by then."

We listened to oldies and talked about our eccentric graduate professors and peers back in Arizona and why higher education had so many well-educated misfits. Both of us had opted to get a graduate degree to advance our goals.

"When we go through the mountains, there may be some snow," Josh added. "That area gets a lot of snow in winter, which is why it's a top world skiing destination. If the road to Yellowstone out of Jackson Hole was open, I'd take you there to see the geysers."

"I'll have to come back."

Climbing the Teton mountain range at first seemed easy, but the higher we went, the thicker the snow, the slower Josh drove, and the more my ears closed. He grew up all over the Northwest and didn't seem all that concerned, but I'd checked the height of this part of the

Rockies on a map and knew the mountains soared over thirteen thousand feet and I was concerned. I'd grown up in the desert hills and had never seen more than a dusting of snow.

"Josh, if you want to turn back, it's fine. I could come back with you on Spring Break and see Yellowstone."

"Nope. I promised you a ski experience and I aim for us to have one."

"Okay, how much further?"

"Just over the mountain," he said.

I hadn't calculated how long it would take us, but near the top, Josh pulled off at a scenic overlook. Because of the snow and lack of visibility, the only scene was of conifer-bearing trees draped in white, like a Christmas card.

A tired snowplow driver had stopped for a rest, and we waved. He rolled down his window and said, "You boys should turn back. Blizzard is coming in this evening, and the highway will close. This is my last run, and the snow is thicker than it has been all winter."

Josh thanked him and took a quick Polaroid of me by the snowplow. Josh drove fifteen miles per hour until the road began to descend. I hadn't been concerned about skidding in his Sunbird and trusted he knew what the car would do.

Soon, we saw the *Welcome to Jackson Hole* sign and found the ski area. Since I had never skied, Josh thought it best we stayed on the bunny slopes. To me, bunny or not, they were nonetheless slopes and only differed in elevation. Navigating the skis were difficult and a workout for my leg muscles. I crossed up skis and tumbled more than once before I got the hang of it. By the time I got the hang of it and had faith I could become better and take on steeper slopes, it was time for lunch. We had buffalo burgers at the Million Dollar Cowboy Bar and sat on horse saddle bar stools. Outside, the arches on the town square were decorated with elk antlers and white Christmas lights. With an overcast sky and snow blowing, it was a beautiful sight to behold, but with the snow becoming heavier and deeper, Josh felt we should get a jump start on the storm.

As we started back up the mountain, I noted Josh was more focused and seemed concerned. What the snowplow had cleared earlier had already been replaced by new snow, and there were no visible tracks on the road from other vehicles. Josh put in a cassette of hymns instead of sixties music as if those singers might cover us with prayer back over the mountain. There were moments when I wasn't clear which side of the road we were on, but I kept quiet. I didn't want my fear to add to Josh's. It seemed to me the only positive part about climbing the mountain road was that we were on the side of the road next to the mountain and trees, so if we slid off road, we wouldn't fall like we might if we were on the side of the mountain that had drops of thousands of feet. Josh had the windshield wipers on high, and before they made it across the windshield, snow covered the glass and the wipers scraped. The heater fan blew and defrosted, but snow iced at the top of the windshield. It was early in the afternoon, but the sky had become dark, the wind was howling, and snow was constant. To top it off, we were cold. Three layers of clothing simply wasn't enough. I would take a sandstorm in the desert or even a thunderstorm over a blizzard on the mountain any day of the week.

As we neared the top, visible tracks had veered off the road on the other side, and Josh said he said he saw lights at an awkward angle in the pines. He pulled to the shoulder, got out, ran through the snow to the edge, ran back, and said, "The snowplow is upside down fifty feet below in trees."

I pulled the antenna out on his oversized 1990s cell phone, but there was no signal and I shook my head. "Nothing."

"You signal anyone to go for help, and I'll get my gear and climb down and try to see if he's alive and if I can help pull him back up," Josh said.

"Be careful," I said, but he was an Eagle scout leader and a volunteer firefighter before he'd come to Arizona for Graduate school, and he knew how to survive. He had the rappelling gear in the Sunbird's trunk and shared he might need my help to pull him to safety. I imagined if Josh couldn't get to him, or we didn't get help, the driver would likely perish in the blizzard. The mountains were cold, unforgiving, and dangerous for the unprepared. I couldn't see Josh after a few minutes, but he heard me yell, "Are you okay?"

"Yeah," he yelled back.

I heard an engine in the distance, hoped they would see my flashlight and the Sundbird's hazard lights flashing, and waved at the driver. He stopped, I told him the snowplow was off the road, upside down, that my friend was trying to rescue him, and the older man told me he was headed to Jackson Hole and would get rescue to come. I did exercises to keep my body warm, was thankful bears were hibernating, and waited what seemed a long time before I heard Josh yell, "I've got him, going to hoist him up." In the distance, I heard another engine, knew the old man had made it, and sent help. Two rescue guys in a four-by-four emergency vehicle pulled alongside Josh's car.

"We're almost there," Josh yelled, and the rescuers pulled an orange stretcher basket from the back of the truck and a medical kit. One of the rescuers climbed over to help Josh pull the snowplow operator to safety while the other told me, "We heard from the County he hadn't returned, but they wanted to give him a little more time."

The snowplow driver had minor cuts and bruises and admitted he wasn't sure what had happened and thought he'd perish. He thanked us several times and the rescuers loaded him. Josh started the Sunbird and drove down the mountain, both of us shivering and craving warmth. When we got to the first gas station and convenience store, we stopped, got coffee, and cleaned the windshield. I looked back at the Teton mountain range in the distance, was thankful to have played a part in a rescue, appreciative to have survived, and nodded in respect to the majesty of nature.

Hospitality

I didn't think much about a group of my daughter's friends coming over after lunch on Thanksgiving to snack and watch a football game, but I intuitively felt her roommate and sorority sister Anna Marie looked at me a little strange. Had I dribbled turkey gravy on my shirt? Perhaps some pumpkin pie at the corner of my mouth or a piece of macaroni and cheese stuck in the groove between my front teeth? I caught a quick glimpse in the hall mirror and knew I at least looked alright.

After her friends left, my daughter Becca said we needed to talk but preferred to wait until the next morning over coffee. The next morning, I fretted while my wife put out fresh fruit, granola, and yogurt and made individual cups of coffee using our favorite k-ups.

"I want to talk with you about your pineapples," Becca said.

My wife learned right after we married pineapples signified hospitality and bought several. We had a cement one in the flower bed, a small flag with one embroidered on it near the front door, and even an antique print over the piano that was valuable. Relief washed over me. There was no plan to elope; she just wanted our kitschy décor. "You can have them if you'd like," I said, beaming. "One day they'll all be part of your inheritance anyway."

"I don't want them. Do you guys know what they mean?" she asked.

"Yes, hospitality," my wife replied.

"No, it means you're swingers and you are ready, willing, and able to have some physical recreation with others. It's embarrassing," she said.

"What the hell? Where did you hear that?" I asked.

"My roommate Anna Marie told me, some of my other friends mentioned it, and I think word has gotten around. It's horrifying! One of my friends said maybe you weren't my dad!"

"But we're not swingers," I said.

"These pineapples say otherwise," Becca snapped.

My wife laughed. "Don't be silly."

I directed, "You tell them we're not swingers" and added, "I thought all of that swinging had died off in the 1970s. Regardless, it does give me a great reason to have a yard sale."

"We're not getting rid of anything. It represents hospitality!" my wife said.

"Yeah, but maybe a bit more hospitality than we'd be willing to offer!" I barked.

My daughter stormed off, and my wife said, "Ridiculous," shaking her head and busying herself with laundry.

While there was something flattering about it, I made up my mind that I could get rid of the pineapples, a little at a time. The concrete statue would topple and break, the flag would be ripped by the wind, and the print would fall, shattering the glass. This would all happen over the next few weeks, so it didn't seem so sudden.

Turret

When J.T. Morgan stood on the deck surrounding the circular turret room on top of the Jekyll Club Hotel to smoke a cigar as the sun rose, he didn't notice the shrimp boat passing through the East River into Jekyll Sound before it worked the Atlantic coastline, and he didn't see young Elliot Gould leaving the family cottage to pick Cherokee roses for his grandmother. What Morgan did see in his mind's eye over and over was his daughter Julia on the ground below, blood flowing from her mouth onto the grass and her white summer dress stained.

Whether she jumped because of her father's refusal to allow her to marry Elliot or whether she slipped on the iron railing was never known, but for Morgan and other parents they'd known who lost a child, it's a blow like none other, and after construction of his own cottage was completed, he never stayed in the turret again. He'd told his wife Ann he awoke from a dream where he'd seen Julia looking down, tracing the shell wallpaper in the turret with her pointer finger, circling the turret, and disappearing through the door. Then, he'd seen her circling the Jekyll Club grounds and then out toward the dirt road that circled the island, repetitive circular movements like the design of a conch shell and the universe.

Morgan's overwhelming pain led him to befriend the teen Elliot and even offer him a position in the banking industry, even though he knew the senior Gould wanted him to stick with the railroad industry. Morgan knew that industry would fade over time, that the Wrights were onto something with their attempted flights, and Morgan had opted to invest in technology rather than the railroad. Elliot politely declined, but invited Morgan to accompany him on an island hunting trip the next morning where they'd check Elliot's racoon traps near Driftwood Beach.

As they stepped around the palmetto and Sago palms and fanned the Spanish moss draping Oaks from their faces, Elliot spotted his trap highlighted by the morning light. "Look," he whispered to Morgan. "I've got one."

"Excellent, chap."

"Stay back. I don't want to ruin his pelt with a shot."

Elliot crept forward, took the butt of his rifle and raised it high, and swiftly brought it down onto the head, killing the racoon instantly, but when he propped the butt of the gun on his boot to pull the dead racoon from the trap, the gun discharged right into his abdomen, and the young Elliot simply said, "Oh, no."

Morgan left the gun and racoon and scooped Elliot and moved through the island brush as quickly as he could. He scraped his face, he sweated profusely, and his heart pounded and throbbed in his throat. He reached the Gould cottage and repeatedly kicked the door with his boot.

"Dear God," Mrs. Gould shrieked from behind her servant when he opened the door. She called to her other servant, "Help me." They placed young Elliot on the daybed in the drawing room, tried to stop the gushing blood, and tried to get a call out on the new phone line, but it didn't work as well as it had when Bell had made the first transatlantic call from Jekyll. They sent for the mainland doctor. The servant stood by the grandfather clock's pendulum in the foyer, ready to stop it the moment Elliot passed, but Elliot's youth and stamina won, and Morgan told the servant, "Get away from that clock. He's not going anywhere."

"At least he's still with us," he whispered to himself on the way back to tell his wife about the events. Ann stood on the balcony of the turret wringing her hands after one of the Jekyll Club's employees shared there had been a hunting accident. She couldn't lose him, too, but she had no need for fear. She was reassured when Morgan was back, and they later heard the doctor had removed the bullet, sewed Elliot's wound, and gave him medicine to help heal. That night, Morgan dreamed of Julia circling the turret, the club grounds, and the island until she circled up into the night sky toward a distant star.

A Piece of Pencil Lead

There's a piece of pencil lead in my arm. It's not really lead but graphite. If you glance quickly, you'd assume it was another freckle. Been there forty years and I haven't had cancer. Maggie Freeman punched me by accident in the third grade, scooping up crayons, pencils, and erasers to put in her Barbie tin. It was an accident, but my eyes filled with tears. I wiped them before they rolled. We have our class reunion soon. I wanted to show Maggie as a joke, but she died last year from cancer that spread before they found it.

Alien

I hadn't shut the door or taken attendance when one of the students asked, "Mr. Riley, have you ever seen a UFO?"

"I've seen lights in the sky, but whether it was a bird, a plane, or Superman, I don't know." Some giggled, but I knew better than to tell them that I knew UFOs were real, because the news would spread like stage four cancer, and I'd be out a job at the prep school, union or not, because they can always find a way to get rid of who they want. Truth is, I'd seen a UFO once when I first started teaching at a school in Ruwa, Zimbabwe. Other teachers and many students who were outside at recess had seen it, too. The leaves had shimmied on the trees, and dust rose from the ground. I raised the window but heard no noise. When I saw the kids running toward the stand of trees, I saw the silver saucer and the aliens, just like I'd read in sci-fi magazines. They were gray with spindly arms and legs and had large black eyes. I'd read aliens communicated telepathically, so I had quietly begged to be abducted like Elijah or the hundreds of thousands of others throughout time, but I hadn't experienced the classic symptoms afterward like missing time or gaps in memories. We had been hushed by the administration and law enforcement, and the media chalked the children's accounts up to mass hysteria.

I had, however, often felt like an alien because of teaching seniors who were more obsessed with their grades after the fact and wanted credit repair, a do-over, or some heavenly extra credit but had no interest in learning what they'd done wrong. They seemed more interested in who might fondle who under the table at the prom dinner, who they might take for classes at a college or university depending on which faculty members had chili pepper marks next to their name at ratemyprofessor.com., or which fraternity or sorority they would join based on keg history, which famous legislator had been involved with the Greek organization, or who might go easier on them in court. They were also interested in what reward their parents might bestow on them for their graduation milestone for being dutiful and showing up for twelve years—a new car or trip to Europe.

I was more interested in their graduation, not because of "No Child Left Behind" but because the philosophy most of the teachers felt was more accurate: "Leave Teachers Behind." The only problem was that there was always another class behind the one leaving where someone would get caught swallowing someone's hydrocodone prescription in the restroom with cupped hands full of water or masturbating in a stall and sending sperm swimming through sewer lines with no hope of fertilization, proving once again that everyone gets laid whether it's who one wants or not. After all, Atlanta Rhythm Section's "Imaginary Lovers" always consent. No Title IX or sexual harassment worries there.

"Remember, your summaries on Mesopotamia are due tomorrow," I told them. "So, spend your time wisely working today in class." My words fell among the deaf. Laptops were open to Solitaire games or music videos on screen, people whispered, and some ate high-protein low-carbohydrate bars and washed them down with sugar and caffeine-laced soft drinks. I knew tomorrow I might get some summaries plagiarized from Google links, the modern *World Book*, and the rest wouldn't bother, but they'd pass and graduate because that was the unwritten policy that left no child behind, caused graduation rates to soar, and caused higher education remediation to increase.

I wouldn't be the lone alien stranded in this classroom much longer and crossed off the days on my desk calendar and in my lesson planner. I had one more year to go before retirement, and I looked forward to leaving this world behind and moving onto something else. When I closed my briefcase, pushed the wooden chair under the desk, and turned off the lights, I walked down the hallway and outside. I thought I saw something block the sun and reflect light, heard a faint whooshing sound, and saw a dust devil in the distance. I hoped the aliens had finally returned for me after all these years and dropped to my knees, put my briefcase down, and folded my hands pyramid-style to pray they'd take me, but I heard laughter and realized some of the students were flying a drone in the parking lot. I figured they were spying on the girl's swim team at the pool.

Ten Commandments

The organist played soft music at All Saints, and I took a seat close to the back. I liked to be the first to exit. I felt relaxed and wondered why I didn't come more often. I was a good person, believed, and obeyed the commandments, but most of the time, I slept late, watched the news, and sipped coffee. I didn't like wearing church clothes either. The stained-glass windows with sunlight filtering color onto the walls, the decorative columns, scrolls carved on ends of wooden pews, and statues of saints on the walls were holy reminders and functioned to pull me back to my boyhood when I was sinless.

As I listened to the music, I wondered about my stocks, if the recent change in politics would have a negative impact on the market or if it might increase. All my adult life, I had focused on making money, piling up treasures for senior years like my cabin in the finger lake district, my convertible Audi, and my art collection that doubled in value, except one painting that god-damned art dealer scammed me on. I lost fifty thousand dollars, and if I found him, I'd kill him and maybe spray paint the son-of-a-bitch to look like that abstract fake art.

I wondered if my parents could see me from heaven or purgatory or wherever. They'd be proud I'd made it back to All Saints. Even though they'd stayed humble and faithful, they'd also stayed poor. I was living-damned-proof one could make it financially and still attend. I probably should've given them more when they were in that nursing home, when the nursing home folks took their inner-city shack of a house because Medicaid wasn't enough to cover the bills. I should have gone to see them more, but I hated the smell of urine in that facility. I had told them I had to work, and they believed me.

Parishioners had shuffled in All Saints and plopped in their same pew I recalled from childhood, and I caught a side view of Samantha joined by her bald and bloated husband plus three kids. Side view wasn't bad and either she'd had a nip, tuck, and boost here and there, or she'd been working out. I wanted to slip her my business card and fantasized we would meet up and rekindle our friendship with benefits. I wondered if her family had the new Land Rover SUV by the curb outside. I'd toyed with the idea buying one.

The minister read some passages about forgiveness, there was some special music, and an offering was collected, but I'd left my wallet in the car. I fanned the deacon away, tried to stay awake during the special choir music, but slipped out as soon as I could, flashed a quick wave to Samantha, and figured I'd try to call her. I reasoned that visit would hold me over for some time, and I'd try to come back to All Saints come Christmas.

The Rejection

The rejections did not come on the stereotypical Monday but rolled in like a tsunami on Tuesday without any alert and made me feel slammed and tossed about in the water like a compact car caught up in the powerful wave. I thought I had grown immune to rejections over the years and had trained myself not to let them get to me, but when I had a record eleven in one day, I realized that I hadn't grown immune to them and wanted to lash out whether at the lazy someone in the office who didn't pull his weight but sat on it in a cozy chair, a random car flashing the left blinker when there was nowhere to turn on the commute home, or at my neighbor's yapping dog who has yapped at me every afternoon for the past eight years, but I did not lash out.

I worked my rationalizations like someone on an assembly line, putting together a Lego-like product: "You know they all get published eventually", "You know you write well or you wouldn't have been nominated by editors for three Pushcarts or had been a finalist in that London contest", and "Remember, you did land in one of the top magazines in the United States that's considered a career changer even though your career didn't change since people don't read a lot unless the writing is about someone already famous and who doesn't need the money to put his son through a public university, make house payments, and pay off his own student loans."

After my wave of rationalizations, I plopped in the recliner and watched reruns of *All in the Family*, *Sanford and Son*, and *Everybody Loves Raymond*, but I was too upset to laugh at Archie and Edith, Fred and Aunt Esther, or Frank and Marie, though I imagined Marie would be an excellent editor given her critical nature. I reread the note from the editor of *The Lynbrook Literary Review* who wrote, *We appreciate the opportunity to read your work. Although we do not have a place for your submission please know that we appreciate the hard work you put into it.*

First, I admitted to myself the note was nice enough, but that wasn't the point. I had received hundreds, maybe thousands, of rejections, some of which were even nicer and personal. No, the point here wasn't even that the rejection was missing a comma after the introductory material. What got my goat, as my departed English teacher grandmother would have said, likely while reading from a classic propped on her breasts, was that I didn't have a story being considered by them.

I had made errors before. I sent a simultaneous submission to a journal and it was accepted elsewhere. I sent a kind note to the editor who blasted me for withdrawing and asked that I not submit again. Also, I couldn't withdraw a story from one literary magazine because I honestly couldn't read my own handwriting since I recorded everything by hand and refused to learn Excel to track submissions. I also hated to admit that I was not the best reader of guidelines and sent a story to a journal that only takes submissions from lesbians, trans, or BIPOCs. I'd received a kind note back from the editor asking if I would mind sharing how my WASP point of view might fit.

When I searched my deleted files with Lynbrook's email address, I found the submission from ten months ago, followed by my withdrawing one of the submissions within a month and the second within two months. Both submissions had been accepted elsewhere, and Lynbrook finally sent me an email rejection after I had specifically withdrawn both stories. I'd had enough. Lynbrook wasn't *The New Yorker*, for goodness sakes, and even they give you a ninety-day window. I thought about posting their insanity on Facebook, Twitter, Instagram, or LinkedIn, but I had heard from other writers I might get black balled, that they'd heard it happened to others who were honest and voiced concerns freely and openly. I thought about what I did with repeated phone calls on my land line from spammers trying to extend my car warranty on my ten-year-old vehicle I've almost completely rebuilt, but the air horn won't work with *The Lynbrook Literary Review* because they don't show a telephone number on their Weebly website.

The next morning, I decided to do nothing. I didn't respond to the rejection (I wondered how many months it would take them to read a response, and by then, I might have landed the same story they rejected in a big one and received another Pushcart nomination). I decided to scribble *I withdrew these stories before they rejected them* on the printed rejection and file it. I mused my kids wouldn't read it either once I was gone, and they were left to recycle the contents of my filing cabinet, close my email account, and donate my belongings to Goodwill.

Smoking in a Storm

The Scotia Prince cruise ship out of Portland, Maine rocked back and forth in the storm, and neither of us were comfortable, nor slept well, in the ship's Lilliputian beds. To step on deck for a smoke was frightening, but the gnawing in my body for nicotine overruled. I made my leg muscles stiff and braced against the wall of the cabin, cupped my hands to light the cigarette and then unlocked my leg muscles and used my free hand to grip the door frame The rain pelted me and my cigarette, and for some reason, I remembered being a toddler in my wind-up swing crying because rain pelted me, thunder scared me, and my diaper was wet and smelled of ammonia, but my babysitter had been more concerned about her fingernail color than my rash.

I didn't smoke half of the cigarette, threw it down, and the ship lunged forward over a wave and then down, and I slipped trying to get back in the door. Fortunately, I didn't slip the few feet to and through the guard rail, where I imagined great whites waited below. Little did I know that sharks would be the least of my worries. My expert dog paddling skills wouldn't have lasted long enough to be thrown a life preserver, and I might not live long enough to see the ship disappear beyond the horizon.

My wife was in the closet the ship said was a bathroom seasick and hugging the stainless-steel toilet like we had done in college after a keg party. She had thrown up the free buffet and was in the throes of dry heaves. She probably wouldn't have come to search or called for help until I'd sunk below. I imagined I may have been mentioned in the Yarmouth, Nova Scotia or Portland, Maine newspapers in the back near the classifieds or maybe in my hometown paper back in Tennessee. I imagined my wife would collect enough insurance to start over, to find someone who didn't smoke or have my flaws of frugality, anxiety, and an overly imaginative mind, but rather than give in, slide, and belly flop into the cold sea below, I mustered all the strength I had and pulled myself back inside, slamming the vinyl coated Styrofoam door shut. I decided to throw policy overboard and smoke in the restroom with the exhaust fan running.

As the bad weather subsided and the sun rose, we forgot about the storm, the seasickness, my almost slipping overboard, and even childhood memories swirled back into the deep recesses of my mind. We had coffee on the deck and watched seals frolicking and whales exhaling mist. As Yarmouth came into view in the Bay of Fundy, I felt we were sailing into an ancient painting with green cliffs against the dark sea, brightly painted cottages dotting the landscape, and a swarm of gulls that would make a Hitchcock fan duck and cover his head. As we lugged our suitcases without wheels a half mile to the hotel, we quickly learned the exchange rate was against us and our cash would not last the week, but I enjoyed smoking while we picked up sea glass on the beach by the lighthouse, while I watched fisherman unload lobster, and in the cemetery by the statue of our lady of Fatima who didn't weep for me like she had so many tourists.

Elevator Ride

When I met Sara at the music fest in Washington Square, I had no idea our breath would mingle in the winter air, like the verse from "Diamonds and Rust" that immortalized a relationship between Baez and Dylan, and I had no idea that mingling would lead to our being engaged in Lake Placid six months later. We hiked one thousand feet from our bed and breakfast nestled among the Adirondacks, and I gave her my grandmother's wedding ring.

I grabbed her arm when she jumped up and down. "Be careful." I imagined if she fell off a cliff and died, they would think I'd pushed her.

"I'm just so happy," she said. She held out her arm, the diamond glistened, and she shouted, "It's beautiful." The sound echoed a few times in the distance.

"It was my grandmother's," I said. "I hope you don't mind."

"That just makes it more special," she said. "She had a phenomenal life."

"Yes," she did. "She worked for two first ladies and a governor."

"Did she ever share any great secrets?"

"No. She had too much class. Never would have written a book for money. She wanted to make a difference. It's not like that now."

"True," she said.

As we stood and gazed at the low clouds on the distant peaks, I imagined the height was level to my office in the Empire State building back in the city, but that day, I relied on my hiking boots to get down without slipping, not an elevator gliding a thousand feet in mere minutes with me wearing a suit and Italian leather shoes.

When I first landed the job in the city out of Dartmouth, I never thought I'd be working in such an iconic building, the same building my great aunt Betty had worked in as an elevator operator in the 1940s. An Army bomber plane had hit the building in thick fog, and she plunged seventy-five stories. Aunt Betty hadn't been killed even though she'd suffered burns and breaks. I think about her every day

I come and go from the building, especially when I feel a sudden jolt in the elevator's cable system, but I don't share my connection to Aunt Betty out of superstition. I wondered if she'd met famous people when they visited like Drew Barrymore I'd seen or what she thought when she heard there was a jumper.

Sara and I talked briefly on our cells each day to discuss wedding details at St. Patrick's between spreadsheet work, Zoom meetings with overseas investors, and interviews for a new shared Human Resources position between three companies on our seventy-eighth floor. Most of the work like benefits and payroll were outsourced, but the new hire would function as a liaison to those areas as well as be responsible for onboarding and dealing with any issues in the three offices. Even though the businesses differed considerably—a watch company, a social services organization, and a foreign investment firm—it seemed logical to share services.

One young lady, a newly-minted NYU business graduate from rural New York who wanted to stay in the city, finished her interview with me and seemed to be turned around. I told her I'd show her the way out, that the building could be confusing and overwhelming to first timers, so we walked to the elevator. We almost passed up the ride when it stopped, since it looked crowded, but a guy from upstairs in an airline office said they could squeeze two more inside.

We packed in like sardines, and I watched the floor buttons light up and ding. After a few, there was a loud pop above and the elevator plummeted. My heart pounded in my chest and head, and I felt sweat beads drip in my eyes from my forehead. Lights and dings became faster and faster, and since I was in the front by the doors, I pressed the palms of my hands to the aluminum covers and planned to jump up a few inches when the elevator hit bottom, since I figured it might prevent bone breaks upon impact, if I lived at all. I thought of my great aunt Betty, of Sara, but before we hit bottom, the elevator moved back up and then down like an extreme bungee experience until it came to vibrate like a slinky on two different stairsteps.

A voice came over an intercom. "Everyone alright?"

"Yes," the airline employee said. "But I imagine several of us now need to use the restroom."

"Currently, you are between floors four and three, and we will manually lower you to the third. The doors will then open, but please stay calm. The cable jumped its track. It may be the elevator is too full." I felt my face flush, but I knew the airline employee should feel as guilty, too, for his invitation.

Within a few minutes, facility workers had the doors open and people exited, having a 1200 feet per minute fall story to share with their families, friends, and co-workers, but since no one was killed or injured, it wasn't nearly as gruesome as jumper Evelyn McHale's. She had leaped to her death but landed completely intact on the roof of a limousine. A suicide note in her coat pocket announced she wouldn't make a good wife for anyone and the story had made *Life* magazine and an Andy Warhol print. I told the Human Resources candidate she'd get the job, if the elevator ride hadn't scared her off, and she accepted.

I'd met Sarah later for dinner in Manhattan but decided not to tell her about my elevator ride, since we planned to have a reception in an entertainment space that had an observation deck on the seventy-eighth floor. The observation deck for our reception had been the one where some suicide jumpers had landed if they didn't jump out far enough out to fall all the way to the street below and were surprised their suicide wasn't successful when they were hauled off to hospitals for shock therapy and a lifetime of pills.

It occurred to me after my Yellow Cab ride that an elevator ride was much safer, given the driver had jumped the curb twice and had shaken his fist and screamed at another cab driver, the yellow cars only inches apart. I kissed Sarah at the hostess counter, and as we took our seats and ordered drinks, she said "You know, I'm not sure everyone will be comfortable with a reception at the Empire State building. It's really high up."

"With the free liquor we're providing, I would think they would feel very comfortable."

"Good point," she responded.

"But if you want to change the venue, I'm okay with that. It's not the height they are afraid of, you know. It's death."

"Or maybe it's not death so much as it is the fear of the unknown."

"Maybe, but you just have to go with things. Like marriage. We don't know what it'll be like, but we're going through with it."

"True," she said. "Let's just leave it there. If they don't want to come after the wedding, they don't have to."

"More liquor for others."

Sara laughed, took my hand, glanced at my grandmother's former ring that dazzled in the candlelight, and said, "Everyone loves diamonds."

"But not rust," I said.

"What?"

"Nothing," I replied, smiled, and signaled the waitress we were ready to order.

A Writer's Trophies

Alex had dug up irises in the driveway at Faulkner's Rowan Oak with a spoon and had them in a clay pot on his desk. The rocks from Flannery O'Connor's flower beds were paper weights, and a nice piece of pottery held peacock feathers he'd picked up on the grounds at Andalusia and rested on the other corner of his desk. He had some wood planks from a whitewashed picket fence from Robert Frost's farm in Massachusetts. He'd constructed a picture frame that held a black and white photo of Robert Frost reading at Kennedy's inauguration. He had some of Sylvia Plath's baking dishes from a secondhand shop in England, but the strangest of all was the stuffed cat with six toes he'd put on a shelf. The cat he'd found in the alley at Hemingway's home was one from the herd in Key West, and he put it on ice in an Igloo cooler until he could get it to the taxidermist.

When they found him slumped over the desk in the office, the EMTs helped the funeral home load him in the hearse. One said, "Must've been a nut. Takes all kinds, I guess."

"No," the other said. "Just eccentric. Taught writing part time for the college. Left all this to them is what I heard."

The development officer met the English department head the next week to assess the gift, but neither saw much value, except the house, which might provide a handful of endowed scholarships to writing or literature students after the investment yielded earnings in three to five years, depending on the market, but the rest would be picked up in a box truck by Goodwill.

Students searching for retro clothes and unique decorations for dorm rooms, fraternity and sorority houses, and apartments in the weeks ahead didn't think much of any of his junk dispersed among the former treasures, and most found the six-toed cat appalling. The manager of Goodwill who had an English degree from the college saw Goodwill as a gigantic bird's nest. She told one customer, "Birds gather all this stuff to make their nests, and we do the same thing. It's just that this nest is five thousand square feet."

The manager decided she'd take Hemingway's six-toed cat but wondered what had become of Alex's publications or Word files of stories he'd been drafting and submitting. She wondered where the ideas of writers go if they don't get published. She imagined there was another cloud like the technology one where the ideas go, and then periodically, those ideas rain down and are recycled on the next generation.

Keys

Brenda was like a leer jet, fast and focused with a smooth and graceful landing after a daily journey, and she'd loved Mike since kindergarten at the Episcopal day school. He'd given her a cut out red heart Valentine and a small box of candies stamped with messages back then that read *Be Mine Forever, Everlasting Love, Your Valentine.* On the back were chubby Cupids shooting arrows. Neither of them even knew what the messages meant.

After high school, both went to Virginia, and he majored in pre-med and stayed for medical school. She majored in Education and taught grade school. They married right after graduation at Monticello, where Thomas Jefferson had lived, though their ancestors would not have approved the location since they had connections back to Adams. His place had been rented for two months in advance. She was pregnant with the first of three girls, and Mike worked long hours, partly to meet the rising patient demand, partly to support them, and partly to stay away from all the hormones and drama, though his body language and comments never revealed which.

When Brenda's life got busy with the girls, teaching, and the PTO liaison and Mike got busy with the practice, experiences of holding hands and skating to Sinatra's "Moon River" under the strobe light, or early Sunday mornings listening to a Sinatra album and her dancing in a gown and Mike in PJs to "All of Me" in the kitchen, became distant memories.

One Monday, Brenda came to school, shuffled papers in the lounge by the mailboxes, paced the halls scanning the tile floors and baseboards, and grabbed random students by lockers to see if they'd seen her keys. She went into the office and asked the school administrative assistant and told another teacher to watch her homeroom while she searched outside. Finally, the principal walked out and asked her if she'd left them in her station wagon. She smirked at him, told him she hadn't lost it but was close, and they walked closer to check. Brenda was mortified her station wagon was still running, keys in the ignition.

"Is everything alright, Brenda?"

"It will be fine," she smiled.

That night, she reminded Mike of their shared past, their family, and the life they'd built together, and she told him if he wanted to give it all up for his nurse, he could, but he'd better think long and hard about how he'd start over with nothing, how he'd have to explain his mistakes to the medical board that she'd helped him cover, how he pushed drugs that didn't work for vacations in the islands, and how he'd put real estate in his underaged daughters' names with elderly parents as co-signers to avoid the capital gains taxes.

On Tuesday evening, Mike brought home a heart-shaped box of chocolates, a card, some fresh flowers, and put in a CD of Sinatra in the player on the counter, and they slow danced and he told Brenda he was sorry. She patted his back like she was burping a baby and told him it would be alright, that they would work it out.

Jim Moore Restoration

The signage on the back and sides of the box truck read *Jim Moore Restoration.* I read it at the traffic light at 5:00 a.m. and wondered what Jim Moore was restoring that early. I hadn't slept well and was headed to my office in an older part of town that was sketchy at best. The sign reminded me of an uncle I had named Jim Moore who was a drunk. He was drunk when he'd been the third husband of my aunt, he was drunk when he painted houses, and he was drunk when he put me in his Ford Ranger and drove to a pond, where he talked about how fish were attracted to fresh worms, not stale ones, just like women he'd said, and he pointed, grabbed at my shorts, and laughed at a joke that only he got. He'd left my aunt for a painting job in Atlanta, and I wondered if he was still alive, had started his own restoration business, got rid of his Ranger, and bought a box truck. I imagined he hadn't since that was more effort than a drunk would put forth.

When the box truck stopped at the next light, I swerved in behind it to be in the turn lane. Whether it was the streetlight or the light rain, I thought I saw the back panel bump out and then in as if something in the box was moving around. I followed the box truck to Angel Apartments on Hollywood Street, a road I didn't like driving on because of the drug busts, shootings, and stabbings, but I figured criminals weren't up at 5:00 a.m. The truck turned on its blinker and pulled in, and a couple of cars, with smoke coming from their tailpipes, idled next to each other. The box truck pulled in front of them and stopped.

I wondered if something sinister was transpiring but dismissed my imagination. I swerved to avoid killing a cur dog and eased into a convenience store parking lot and circled back. I stopped, grabbed my phone, and told the 9-1-1 operator about Jim Moore's truck. She said she heard the Angel family was remodeling their apartment complex, but there was an officer in the neighborhood, and she'd have him check just to be sure. I drove on to my office and figured they'd chalk my call up to another hysteric busy body in town, but mid-morning, I read the newspaper's headlines in my Facebook feed and learned a human trafficking bust that saved five teens had occurred at the Angel Apartments, thanks to the unknown hero caller.

I didn't think I was a hero and didn't call to identify myself either, but I was glad to read in the interview that owner Jim Moore fired the employee who borrowed the box truck. The newspaper quoted him: "Said he was going to move his mama. I'm sure his mama would be disappointed."

Rodeo Drive

Among the G-Wagons, Ferraris, and Rolls Royce convertibles, we parked our rented Ford Escape and walked with tourists and the rich and famous shoppers. My wife pronounced it "Ro-day-o" while I pronounced it "Ro-dee-o" because I was from the rural Midwest and had gone to rodeos my entire life. My pronunciation annoyed her, and she poked me in the chest with her newly-painted yellow fingernails, told me to keep that to myself, and try to act like I wasn't a redneck. For her, shopping was as much pretend as it was when she played with dolls, performing role play on the shag carpet of her childhood bedroom.

We saw some pro sports players (I knew who they were), rappers (my teens knew who they were), and actors (my wife knew who they were) as we dashed in and out of the major designer stores: Gucci, Barberry, Christian Dior, and many others. We didn't, however, bother any of them for autographs or selfies. We'd learned from having backstage passes and getting to meet singers in Branson that while all of them appreciate their fans, many of them were shy and had a close circle of family and friends. They shied away from cameras and reporters when they were on "their time" and often tried to hide their identities with sunglasses, hats, and in some cases, wigs, or hair pieces. They lived behind gates in multi-million-dollar homes, had extensive security systems, and often had security guards while we lived in a two hundred-thousand-dollar ranch home in a neighborhood that was in a state of decline and had a security system from a box at Wal-Mart.

My daughter wanted to go into the Gucci store while my wife wanted to go into the Christian Dior store. After one look at a multi-colored sweater with strings pulled over a partial mannequin in their window with a price tag of over a thousand dollars, I told her to go ahead, and I would go to the Gucci store with our daughter. We had to stand in line for thirty minutes until a salesperson was available to assist us, but I didn't need assistance because I wasn't buying anything. I think the least expensive product in the store was a pair of flip-flops (I think they were labeled sandals), and they cost five hundred dollars. It occurred to me the individual in China who manufactured them probably made less than one dollar per day and that was a considerable mark up and profit for the owner. Besides, the day I spent five hundred dollars on flip-flops would be the day my wife could send me on to an asylum for the capitalistic insane.

I talked with a guy who seemed normal in front of me, and he had a sidebar with one of the employees who had her cell and pulled up the items he was there to purchase, not for himself but for his nameless and invisible employer who'd sent him on errands. I tried to tease it out of him, but he didn't bite. When we finally made it to the front of the line, I said hello to the security guard, shared I felt like he'd seen plenty of famous Hollywooders, and he nodded that he had. I asked who had been the most recent one he'd seen. He responded that they were unable to share that information.

We looked around the Gucci store, but in all, I'm certain we weren't in the store more than ten minutes. A saleswoman, however, followed on my heels to make certain I wasn't a thief. Not only did being there reinforce how poor and insignificant I was when compared to stars, I felt like a suspect or a potential criminal. I'd take my lower middle-class poverty and rural Midwest life over big city issues any day of the week.

When we all met up in the Burberry store, their employees also had the doors propped open and we thought we heard firecrackers, but we quickly discovered what we'd heard was gunfire. We saw two large men in suits and dark sunglasses huddle around someone my daughter said was a rapper named DMZ (named for the Korean demilitarized zone, but I had heard the lyrics and pulses through our hallways and floors back home and knew there was nothing demilitarized about them). The bodyguards pushed the rapper into a G-wagon and sped off while police surrounded the block and searched for the attempted assassin. The police didn't locate him, and though I knew we certainly weren't targets, I shared we should move on and visit tourist sites before the day was over. We headed back to our room at the Roosevelt Hotel in Hollywood, a seventh story room with a view of the iconic Hollywood sign, where we would change into more comfortable shorts, t-shirts, and flip-flops and move like zombies into the masses along the star walk.

Taking up Serpents

Her husband said that if the snakes had been well-fed before Sunday service, they likely wouldn't bite as many of the members who came to the country church outside Sand Mountain, Alabama. Laura Francis hadn't grown up as part of a holiness church that believed in taking up serpents, and she didn't believe what she figured to be a misinterpretation of biblical text, but Sam had hypnotic green eyes, a lumberjack body, and had slithered into her life.

Once they married, part of her responsibility was lifting the mice by their pink tails from their aquarium and dropping them into the snake aquariums. His responsibility was combing the mountain sides, searching under rocks for copperheads, listening for rattlesnakes, and capturing them in a burlap sack. She didn't mind feeding them, but she told Sam that she wouldn't take up serpents in or out of church. She perched on a stool and watched them slither through the wood chip bedding and swallow the mouse whole, their mouths expanding, and then seeing the whole mouse inside their distorted bodies. Occasionally when mice weren't in stock, she had to feed baby chicks to the snakes. The fluffy yellow chirpers weren't nearly as easy to watch get swallowed because Laura Francis knew they had potential to grow and provide eggs. Mice didn't seem to have a purpose that she could distill.

Laura Francis sat on the third row in church, far enough away from the front to avoid the gyrating spirit-filled members who in their fit of dancing might drop a snake or lose their grip, from where their thumb and pointer finger pinched the triangular head from each side, and fling it to the floor or into the up-close audience. When one landed and coiled on the pine pew where she had been sitting, she stood and rocked back and forth into the aisle to the beat of the music of drums, piano, guitar, and banjo. Laura Francis was a quick study and threw her arms and hands up into the air and danced backward to the last row until the music stopped, and Sam wiped sweat with a white handkerchief he kept in his pocket. Then, she took a seat on the back pew and never moved back to the front on successive Sundays. When Sam questioned her over supper one night, she told him. "I feed them and that's all I'm going to do."

The next week, Sam rattled the cages and told the members, "Laura Francis feeds these snakes, and they are getting fatter and happier." Laura Francis didn't know if a snake could be happy, but she knew that Sam was hoping to stave off any questions from church members about her faith since Laura Francis had moved to the back row and hadn't handled snakes.

When Sam was loading the cages for church one Sunday, he was bitten. Laura Francis rushed him to the emergency room, but the venom quickly spread through Sam's body. Within two days, he died, the congregation gossiped about his faltering faith, and there was a small funeral at the church. One of the members came to get the snakes and the mice and take them to his farm, and Laura Francis listed their land and small house on the mountain for sale. She moved to Huntsville and joined the Episcopal church, where the only things she would take up would be the Bible, the hymnal, and the communion wafer and wine chalice.

Gobekli Tepe

When a herder discovered the tip of a pillar protruding from the tell, his intuition told him it was important, and village officials contacted an archaeologist. Like kids with shovels in a sandbox, the university team moved dirt from the tell and found more pillars in circles with carvings of animals not indigenous to the deserts of Turkey like geese, armadillos, and gazelles. Speculation was the animals came from the ark at nearby Ararat after the flood. Later, the circular ruins seemed to align with one star, a star where NASA noted activity. Perhaps the ancient nomads had attempted contact with their ancestors, or perhaps this was a religious place when the desert was fertile and alive.

All I knew is that I got a basic stipend for this internship, a discount from inflated tuition and fees, and a tent in which to live where I ate mush with a side of desert sand. If sand grew, I'd be a mound myself because it was everywhere--caked in my nostrils, on my eyelashes, around my lips. In the distance, I heard gunfire and bombs explode near the Syrian border where they fight for sand and control in the name of a God, and I was conditioned to sleep by the loud lullaby. In fact, when the war zone was quiet, supplies were low, or troops were on the run, I tossed and turned.

One graduate assistant, an Indiana Jones type with stylish readers, a safari hat, and a knife on his belt, signaled me. "Hey, there, can you bring a trowel and brush? There now, work around this and then brush it." I followed his lead, and we pulled a three-inch figurine from the dirt.

"By God," he said. "It's the first time this little fellow has seen sun and sky in over ten thousand years. You think it was a child's toy, some idol worshiped, or a good luck talisman?"

"I don't know," I said, and quite frankly, I didn't care. It wasn't finders keepers. The whole kit and caboodle was horoscope to me. It could have been this or that, it could have meant this or that, but reality is what we make it, and the graduate assistant would create his own. Yes, it was fascinating and would land him in a journal no one would read, or he could slip it in his pocket and sell it on the black market to pay his tuition and fees, or he could get a feather in his safari hat for donating it to the Turkish museum and have a story to tell his undergraduates for the next thirty years until retirement and then recount it to his nursing home buddies. All I knew for certain was we weren't six feet into this circle of pillars, we had been here an entire semester, I looked and felt like an unwrapped mummy, and I craved a real shower, some clean clothes, a good filet, and some European wine.

Licking the Beaters

The September corn moon was full and bathed our yard and house in light, and my mom busied herself in the kitchen and poured eggs, sugar, butter, milk, vanilla, and flour in a metal bowl. The beaters spun in unison in opposite directions and mixed everything together for my birthday cake from scratch. Mom waltzed from the mixer to the pantry to the cabinets to the oven and back in her yellow polka dot dress draped in a Betty Crocker apron. Mom had Betty's smile, and she wore flour on her fingertips that she sprinkled in her hair when she pressed her Jackie Kennedy hair back in place.

"Daniel, do you want to lick the beaters?"

Licking the beaters was always the foreplay before the climax of eating the birthday cake and waiting until the next day was as bad as anticipation on Christmas Eve.

I gazed through the window and imagined my mother outside in the reflection of moonlight next to the Crape Myrtles and whispered, "I want to lick the beaters," and she holds one out for me, dripping in the sugary cream. I stick my tongue out to catch the heavenly concoction.

"What the hell are doing, Daniel?" my wife said.

I can't tell my wife that Mom is out there inviting me to lick the beaters because she's been gone for years. "Nothing," I replied.

She's dressed in a black pen striped business suit, a white shell, and has readers on. She looks smart and sharp. She'll make a commercial real estate deal that will give us commission enough to get out of credit card, student loan, and mortgage debt. "What kind of birthday cake do you want me to pick up from the grocery store on the way home?"

"Doesn't matter. They're all the same. You pick what you like best, and I'll eat it."

Yellow Wood

When our plane landed in Manchester, New Hampshire, the airport seemed empty. We picked up the keys to our rental Jeep at the kiosk and headed to the garage with our pull luggage. Our first stop was "Mystery Hill" or "America's Stonehenge" just a few miles from Robert Frost's farm. We were the only visitors, and there were two stone paths in the yellow wood, and while we took the one to the left, we vowed we'd also take the other one at some point, leaving no path untraveled.

We heard birds squawking, calling, and singing, and we watched the sun's rays through the trees and leaves and noted the mist rising from warming temperatures. We didn't quite understand why the stones had been placed the way they had been and wondered how different it must have looked four thousand years ago when the Celts constructed the site in perfect alignment with solar and lunar events. We couldn't imagine how they used ancient tools to hack their way through rock to leave their ancient language as a marker and placed the stones perfectly on ley lines to capture and harness the earth's magnetic energies in the crystal embedded rocks. Native Americans left the oral tradition that the structures were already there when they moved here, just like the Native Americans had said to early European visitors about the giant stone compass left on top of Stone Mountain outside Atlanta, Georgia.

Maggie opted not to lie across the rock because it was purported to have been used in sacrifices, but I didn't mind. If the giant, flat rock had historically helped shelter town paupers underneath, had helped hide escaped slaves to go North to Canada, and had been used in some religious ceremonies by Celts like the brochure said, then I felt pretty good absorbing some of that history might be a good thing.

Maggie explored while I laid there, closed my eyes, and let images come. I'm not sure how long I rested on the rock, but when I felt wetness on my lip and chin, I sat up, wiping blood. I allowed the blood to land on the stone rather than get it on my shirt, held my head back, and called for Maggie. She stepped around some boulders and said, "I'm sorry. Did you call my name? I was talking to that older gentleman."

"Who?"

"The caretaker." She pointed toward one of the underground shelters where he'd gone, but I didn't see anyone.

"Nosebleed," I said. "We should get going if we are going to visit Frost's farm and the Salem witch trial site before heading over to Plymouth.

"Okay," she said.

As we made our way down the hill by the other stone path, I asked, "So, what did the caretaker have to say?"

"Funny, I don't recall, really. He turned, pointed, and spoke in a muffled tone."

"What was he pointing at?"

"The lights."

"What lights?"

"Well, there were these round lights off in the distance. I don't recall much more. I was captivated by his long, red hair. I couldn't see it fully because of his robe. His costume really adds to the ambiance of his role as caretaker."

When Mike and Maggie returned to their Jeep, they realized they'd been at the site for six hours when it had only seemed like twenty minutes. They felt rushed and didn't say much on the drive to Frost's farm. Mike didn't have any other nosebleeds, but he did have a slight headache. Later that night at their hotel in Plymouth, they both had dreams of lights and medical procedures, and woke up in a panic at the same time.

"You won't believe my dream," Mike said.

"Oh yeah I would," Maggie said. "I was there with you."

Roch

Just outside Montpelier, Vermont, I went ice fishing at Chapels' Pond. The ice seemed thick, but I slipped and fell, legs plunging straight through a thin sheet into freezing water. My gloved hand couldn't get a grip enough to pull me out, but my Golden Retriever, Roch, named for the patron saint of dogs, clamped his teeth down onto my coat, sweater, and shirt by the collars, digging his paws' nails into the ice, and slowly hauled me out. I thawed by the fire at home, required no medical treatment, and felt dog was spelled God backwards for a reason.

Dads

My wife had a doctor's appointment and left me home alone with our toddler daughter. The diaper sagged when she wobbled across the room. I swept her up, placed her on the changing table, she kicked, and the brown recycled Gerber carrots, green beans, and plums sprayed the wall, the table, carpet, and my shirt. I couldn't figure the correct placement and adhesive straps so I duct-taped the diaper. I couldn't clean before my wife came home and took phone pics to share with her friends and my mother who responded, "Never reads directions, just like his Daddy."

Flatfooted Fred

At the community pool, flatfooted Fred climbed the ladder on the side, his feet slapping scorched concrete back to the diving board, where he ran into air, kicking and flailing, and plunged in the middle, splashing comfortable, oiled girls in bikinis who screeched liked startled birds.

Point Dume

We were attracted to and decided to visit Point Dume at Malibu, California because of the iconic volcanic cone that had been sacred to the native Chumash and was later used as a guide to steer ships away from underwater rocks close to shore. When we pulled into the parking lot, there wasn't a guard on duty, and since the parking lot was more empty than full, we weren't sure if we should pay the meter ten dollars on our credit card or not. We paid the fee mostly because it looked like others had paid and placed their tickets on their vehicle dashboards. We also paid because we had planned to stay a while and weren't sure if someone might come along and write a ticket.

We noticed there were some beach nesters, feathering their patch of sand with towels, coolers, and umbrellas, and we could smell marijuana mixed with suntan lotion wafting on the sea breeze. A family was having a photo shoot for their sixteen-year-old daughter. She was the only person on the beach dressed in a skirt, blouse, and draped in a glittery sweet sixteen sash. We wished her Happy birthday, and she thanked us while her parents nodded. We noticed the racing motorcycles parked in twos further down by the rock cliffs, the same bikes that raced past us and in between traffic lanes on the Pacific Coast highway, but my heart skipped a beat when I saw a young man rappelling off the volcanic rock cliff, and I shared with my wife I simply didn't believe I would ever do that. My fear of heights had been with me since childhood when my family had climbed a fire tower for a view of the Okefenokee Swamp in Georgia while alligators sunned themselves on land or floated like logs in the tea-colored water.

There was a sand trail that weaved its way through the tapestry of cacti, sage brush, and sea grasses and up to a lookout on the cliff. "Let's go up for the best view," Anne said.

I told her, "Go ahead and I'll catch up," but my wife knew I would likely not climb.

"We'll go slow. Come on," she said.

We moved aside for other hikers, some who seemed to glide through the sand in their hiking shoes and sandals unlike me who stopped and emptied sand and small pebbles from my shoes because of pain along the mostly flat arches of my feet. As the path zig-zagged up the cliff, which increased in elevation and difficulty, there were rusted railings for those who needed assistance. We pushed on, taking breathers as needed, and before too long, I stood on the one hundred feet plateau and saw the waves crashing against the rocks below, spraying anyone or anything in the way. It was a sight to behold with incredible and long-range views of the sea to the horizon, the entire Santa Monica Bay, and even Catalina Island in the distance. The only disappointment was we didn't see the gray whales like we'd hoped.

I recalled seeing *Planet of the Apes* with Charlton Heston (Astronaut George Taylor) and Linda Harrison (Nova), their horse ride along the beach, the partial Statue of Liberty in the shallows by the rocks and recalled Heston's realization that he'd returned home to a civilization that had literally turned upside down, where humankind was no longer at the top of the food chain and in control. For a young boy who heard a lot about nuclear proliferation, the possibilities seemed more real than the simple entertainment factor, but I hadn't realized that mother liberty was papier-mâché and that the scene was filmed at Point Dume like other film and television episodes including *Iron Man*, *I Dream of Jeannie*, and *Baywatch*.

The Chumash tribe had much the same view we had at the top a few hundred years earlier, but their selfies were likely etched in their consciousness while jets had transported us to some of the most beautiful points in the states: Yellowstone, Grand Canyon, Mount Desert Island, the Keys, and others. Our experiential abundance wasn't to be taken for granted, but it likely didn't mean as much as the Chumash's view had.

Our view was interrupted by screams, a rock climber running down the trail, and a motionless body at the bottom of Point Dume's cliff. As we hurried down the trail toward the small crowd gathered, my wife ran ahead to see if her nursing skills might be of value. By the time I arrived, Anne had checked the young lady's eyes, taken her pulse, had her move her arms, and tried to get her to wiggle her toes, which unfortunately, she couldn't do. I had heard Anne talk about accidents enough to know that the young lady had likely broken her back and might be paralyzed. I gazed up the rock cliff and wondered at which point her equipment failed.

After she left in the ambulance someone had called, and after Anne had talked with authorities and her rock-climbing friends, she told me that if she hadn't regained feeling within a certain time frame, the paralysis might be permanent. She added that she may need surgery and injections with STEM cells could assist her in regaining her mobility, though she shared the controversy with using perinatal and amniotic stem cells.

"Did you put the lawn chairs in the back of the SUV?"

"Yeah and a cooler with iced water."

"Let's get them out and enjoy the sun and sound of the waves crashing."

"I had hoped to watch a surfer today, but the sea looks rather calm."

The motorcyclists revved their engines and sped away, the teen and her family left, and the rock climbers had followed the ambulance. The beach wasn't crowded at all, and we enjoyed the sounds and watched beachgoers

Anne elbowed me and asked, "Did you see that spray of water there?"

"No," I said.

"Think it was a gray whale?"

"Maybe."

After a while, Anne said, "Let's beat the crowd to the Malibu pier and have brunch. I'm hungry."

"Sounds good to me." We folded our chairs, and I grabbed the small cooler. "I guess we didn't have to pay that ten-dollar parking fee. I haven't seen anyone checking passes on dashboards."

"True," she said.

"Paying the parking fee, though, was worth it for this beauty," I said.

"Yeah. Hey, I hope that girl will be okay."

"Me too." He took one last look at Point Dume, where so much history unfold and where people enjoyed incredible beauty. He hoped it would continue to inspire future generations.

Intuition

I had worked at the Ramada for five years since I was eighteen and had done everything from checking travelers in and out to repairing air conditioners to plunging clogged toilets. I'd even changed linens and planted flowers in a bed by the lobby. The lobby consisted of a sofa, a couple of chairs, side tables with ash trays, a Gideon Bible, floor lamps, and rental plants that were watered and changed out every other week. The burnt-orange carpet popped in the sunlight and cast a glow on the wooden counter that held a cash register, credit card machine, a folio tray for registrations, and the switchboard. I had my own ash tray behind the desk, and by the end of a double shift, it was full of Marlboro light butts that I dumped in the toilet before the next shift.

From Florida to Quebec to California, I'd checked people in, but I never dealt with anyone who gave me a cold and evil feeling. I'd been cursed by unhappy folks because of noise, air conditioners not cooling enough, or even roaches, but if one travels to the South, it's uncomfortable, and there are more bugs than one can imagine. I had even been flimflammed by construction crew out of a hundred-dollar bill with their back and forths and multiple conversations. I had come up short at the end of the shift and had to put in my own money to balance my cash drawer, so I didn't get written up or fired. But they hadn't made me feel uncomfortable.

When the sedan pulled under the porte-cochère, it was nearly ten o'clock at night, and most travelers were already in their rooms. I could tell the fellow was by himself, and he wore khakis and a light plaid, short sleeve button down shirt. He opened the glass door, asked if I had an available room, and I told him we had a single. He filled out the folio, and I felt chilled like the temperature dropped. His stare seemed blank, there was no light in his eyes, and he felt evil, but he wasn't inappropriate in any way. I asked him if he was heading to Florida and he simply said, "No." He didn't offer any additional information. He gave me cash and said he would leave the key in the room. Even after he left, I couldn't shake the feeling and even told the night auditor about him. "You're probably catching a cold," the auditor said. For some, this would've been the perfect customer, because he didn't talk, ask endless questions about chain restaurants, and ask clerks to repeat words because our Southern accents were charming. I have never felt that way again about anyone I met.

Then, I couldn't do a Google search for him on the internet because the web didn't exist in the mid-1990s. I took the carbon copy of his folio and stuffed it in my pocket and found it in a box of certificates and letters from that time period when I was cleaning the garage. When I looked at it, I remembered the coldness and felt evil reaching out from across time. Though I do hundreds of Google searches a week, I didn't need to do one. I knew the name Jeffrey Dahmer as soon as I saw it but didn't know it then. I always heard one should trust his intuition and I'll never question mine again.

Bitten

I went inside the cool house, sat in the leather chair, and drank iced tea. After a few minutes, the sweat on my t-shirt dried, and I figured I needed to finish trimming the widow's hedges across the street. I didn't know why I had volunteered. Maybe it was because I felt guilty for not doing more when her husband died. We'd taken a bucket of KFC with the trimmings to her house and sent a card. Earlier, when I saw her outside, I'd asked her how she was doing. She'd responded that she was hanging on as best she could, and I'd nodded. That's when I volunteered.

I was thankful the wasps that swarmed out of her Holley didn't sting me when I trimmed the shoots jutting toward the gutters, and by the time I took a break, I had plenty of other scrapes and cuts. My ankle hurt, and I noticed two perfectly-spaced puncture wounds. A couple of blood droplets had dried, and there was redness around my ankle bone.

I was concerned. If I had been bitten by a snake in the widow's landscaping, then it was sudden, so quick, in fact, that I hadn't noticed. If I had been bitten by a venomous snake, I think I would have experienced some symptoms, and given at least three hours had passed since I began the work with no symptoms, I assumed I'd be okay. If I had seen the snake and had not been bitten, I would have run as best I could in my flip flops across the yard back to my house. If I had seen the snake that bit me, I would have had a heart attack on the spot, found myself in the tunnel, moving toward light where I imagined St. Peter looked like the old grail knight in *Indiana Jones and the Last Crusade* and might have said, "You know, we didn't have a choice but to wear sandals back in my day. You had a choice and chose flip flops. You chose poorly."

I googled images of snake bites and the images on my phone matched my bite. I read about non-venomous bites and venomous bites. I realized it could have been either type of snake, but if it had been a venomous snake, then the bite would have to have been a dry bite, one in which a venomous snake didn't inject venom.

That night, I rubbed some antibiotic ointment on the bite and put a band aid on it. I promised my wife I'd wear the rubber boots in the future, not flip flops. In the middle of the night, one of my toenails scaped the other foot, and I flew out of bed.

"What's wrong? Did you hear something?" my wife asked.

"No, my feet touched, and I thought it might be a snake."

"If you wake me up again, you won't have to worry about a snake," she hissed.

Gently Used Boat, Motor, and Trailer

I drove the dirt road around the lake, where family cottages hid in the trees near the lake's edge and where water lapped wooden steps. Occasionally, there was a driveway, sloping down, on a vacant lot where people had planned to build but never quite secured the fortune it would cost and hoped to sell and make profit come time to pay their children's college tuition.

I noted the old Plymouth with a trailer and bass boat with an outboard motor rolling down the hill and heard a splash. When I drove down the path and slid to a stop, I noticed the car had dove headfirst, like a whale, and the trailer and boat were slowly sinking. The splash created a wave that moved toward the lake's center. I jumped out, dove into the lake, and noted the old man holding two children, sinking deeper and deeper. Water had already gushed into the rolled down windows and flooded the car, and their lifeless bodies swayed like water plants, this way and that. The trailer had become unhitched, and I pulled until it lodged on a rock only a couple of feet below the surface.

When I came out, I backed my truck until water covered the back tires, hoisted the winch rope to the boat trailer, and pulled her out salvaging the trailer, boat, and motor. When she was free, I hitched her to my truck. I stopped near an old Gulf station that had the only working pay phone left in the county and called the sheriff's department about the Plymouth, the old man, and two children. I pulled the trailer, boat, and motor home and parked them in the barn behind our house. I told my wife it was payback from a buddy who'd lost a bet at work.

I read the next day in the paper the old man had lost his wife to COVID, his daughter had run off and left the two kids with him, and he couldn't raise them on Social Security and was too proud to take food stamps or Welfare. He'd told a friend, "We'd all be better off somewhere else," but the friend added that he never believed he meant committing suicide. I played scenarios before sleep about whether I could have pulled them lifeless to the shore, done mouth to mouth, and what would have become of them if I had. I stopped thinking about what if and instead focused on what was. I realized that in the face of tragedy, there was opportunity. I donated to the old man's church, named my boat after him, and went fishing that weekend.

Needle Teeth

We begged Daddy to buy a baby gator at the Alligator Farm in Florida. When it bit me, it felt like needle punctures, and I bled on the vinyl seats of our Impala wagon. Daddy pulled off the highway, took me to a doctor, and I got antibiotics. Daddy kept him in a cooler until we got home and released him in the Ohio River. There have been sightings reported over the years, but the media claims it's a log. I know better.

The Scream

It went against nature for a child to die before a parent whether suicide, tragedy, or even severe illness and seemed the ultimate cosmic slap in the face to humanity. No Hallmark cards, words of prayer, food, or donations to charity took away suffering from parents the rest of their lives, but even though the result wasn't death, memories of a traumatic event that caused my son to writhe and scream out in pain jarred me to the core.

Halen had tried baseball and found it too slow and boring. He'd tried soccer, but he wasn't as fast as the other boys on the team. I was unclear how I felt when he decided he wanted to go out for football and play on the line. A sport that required one to wear pads on legs, knees, over the crotch area, shoulders, a helmet on the head, and a teeth guard ought to be an indicator that it was dangerous, but football was the dominant sport in many high schools, colleges, and universities, and in the pro sports' leagues. In fact, I had often felt football was almost like a religion or cult, particularly when fans hadn't played, hadn't gone to the college or university, or hadn't lived in the state where their pro team resided. It seemed odd to me that people would simply affiliate themselves with a football team with no connection at all and then worship that team, flying flags on their houses, sporting tags on their vehicles, and traveling to games to tail gate with others who'd made the same choice. It seemed like a form of religion, where coaches or players were deities, like heroes of the distant past—Achilles, Heracles, or Perseus.

The football field smelled of freshly-trimmed grass and had greened from water and fertilizer. Volunteers had helped the coaches touch up the white lines on the field. The field lights were on, and smoke rose from the barbecue wagon pulled by the booster club's president's Ford F150. The smoke wafted in the air, and if the smell of the barbecue hadn't sparked hunger pangs, then the buttered popcorn smell would. The crowd filtered in, and the stadium stands filled. After the coin toss, we watched the kicker kick the ball to the left. The ball wabbled through the air and then landed on the twenty-five-yard line. The offensive line had a five-yard head start over the standard twenty yards.

My wife Allison watched our son on the line with binoculars. I barely made out his jersey number even with my readers. With each play, there wasn't a lot of movement, just a bunch of players colliding with each other to prevent the quarterback or the running backs from being tackled, to prevent the offense from losing yardage, or to give them enough time to pass the ball. If Allison wasn't using binoculars, she rang a cow bell back and forth in the air or screamed along with the cheerleaders: "2 bits, 4 bits, 6 bits, a dollar, all for the Lions, stand up and holler." The cheer was the same one I recalled hearing in high school over twenty years ago when Allison was on the line in her skimpy uniform and her hair in pigtails, and I wondered why cheer coaches and cheerleaders hadn't developed some new ones.

The game was played between the forty-yard lines on each side and had gone back and forth, too far away for the kicker of either team to score a field goal, but in the last two minutes of the second quarter, there had been a scramble, a mass of bodies pushed on each side, yellow penalty flags were thrown on the field by the umpires, and when the mass of bodies was pulled a part, one player was down.

"Oh my God, it's Halen," she said, grabbing her purse, leaving her seat behind, looking back at me, and yelling, "Come on!" when she had already leaped three or four rows below. I followed, and we sprinted onto the field to Halen.

I heard the coach say, "Try to get up, boy. We need you in the game," but when I got close, I saw blood all over his leg, a piece of something that appeared part of a bone had punctured the skin, and Halen screamed without ceasing, except for short breaths in between. Tears formed in my eyes at the pain he suffered, and Allison cradled him. "You'll be alright, baby. You'll be alright."

The trainer said to the coach, "Call 9-1-1. He's going to need to get to the hospital. This is a bad break."

I looked back, players on both teams had taken knees, and parents in the stands were silent because they'd heard Halen scream, a primal scream unlike his baby cries in the crib, his cries from a fall or cut as a toddler, or even his cries from a wasp sting in the yard on Saturday while throwing the football.

The EMT told Allison, "You can go with us to the ER."

"Meet us there," she said to me.

I nodded and asked another parent on my way to the parking lot, "Can you get our stadium seats and hold on to them?"

"Let us know if you need anything," he said.

When I got to the ER, I hadn't been too far behind the ambulance, and the ER doctor said, "We're going to give him something strong for pain, ice the leg to slow swelling, and make sure he's stable. He'll need surgery, we aren't equipped here to do it, and we're going to have to fly him to Atlanta. I've called ahead and the surgical team will be ready when he lands. One of y'all can go on the helicopter, and I'm sorry it can't be both."

I knew Allison would go. She wouldn't leave his side, and when a traumatic experience occurred, a child was an extension of the mother, her having carried him, birthed him, and breast fed him, and to insert myself into the role would be what it would be like to attempt to take the young of a crocodile, hippo, tiger, a deadly experience.

I made the two-hour drive, and when I got to the hospital in Atlanta, Allison was in the waiting room. "He's in surgery," she said. "He didn't even wake up the whole flight or while they prepped him."

"What did the doctor say?"

"He said it was one of the worst he'd seen, but he thought given Halen is so young, it will heal, and he actually could play again if he wanted to, but he wouldn't advise it."

"How was the chopper flight?"

"I wanted them to give me whatever they had given Halen for pain. The flight was nauseating, and I didn't look out, particularly as we flew into the city among skyscrapers. Even when we landed on the roof, I tried not to look. Kept my eyes focused on Halen."

"I bet."

We sat there for another hour until the doctor came through the swinging doors, pulled his mask and cap off, and said, "Well, it took longer than I thought, but it's done. I think he'll be fine. He's in recovery now, they'll get him to a room, and you can see him. He's going to be pretty delirious and out for a while, and we're going to continue the pain meds for a while."

"Thank you, doctor."

The doctor nodded, turned, and then turned back. "You know, I don't usually caution parents about sports because people are pretty passionate about them, but I think you should seriously think about whether he should play football again."

"Thank you, doctor," I said. He nodded and walked down the hall.

Allison turned to me. "Don't think about making this decision now."

"I'm not," I told her. "If we made the decision now, I know what it would be and I can tell you this. I have never in my life heard him scream like that, but I know I don't ever want to hear our boy scream like that ever again. I now know why my grandmother's younger brother's picture hung on her hallway, how she always talked about Jack. I imagine my great grandmother screamed like Halen did when the Army notified her that Jack was found dead on the beaches of Normandy. She later learned his leg had been blown off in a grenade explosion, and he and so many from his company laid on that beach in Normandy wet and cold and screamed all night among those who were dead or dying. Right now, I'm thankful to have Halen, happy he will be alright, but I'll tell you that I honestly don't want him to ever play football again, just like my own mother never wanted me to go into the Army because of her Uncle Jack, just like my grandmother never did the pledge of allegiance again, and why she never bought anything made in Germany or Japan."

"I don't disagree, and I just want to let Halen be included in any decisions."

"Understood."

I stood at the end of Halen's hospital bed, his leg in a cast and elevated, and Allison pulled the chair close to him, and stroked his hair. Texts had buzzed our phones all night, and social media messages and prayers had poured in like rain to nourish us through the experience. As the sun rose over the city, Halen slept, and Allison dozed.

When Halen was out of the hospital, we adjusted to life in a temporary wheelchair before we graduated to crutches. We pushed him onto the sidelines to watch his friends play football. One parent told me, "I stood in the stands and boo-hooed for you, Allison, and Halen as if he were my own son. I dreamed about him, heard his haunting scream, and there wasn't anything I could do. I don't wish that scream on any parent."

"Thank you," I said and knew we'd soon have to have the conversation about playing football next year. Like the first ride on a bicycle, a first day at school, or a first drive alone, I couldn't always be there to protect him or save his life, and I believe our worrying about children is what ages us more quickly than those who don't have children.

Mandela Effect

After five o'clock, we got together at La Siesta for margaritas, fajitas, and tacos to celebrate Cinco de Mayo, and someone asked what the holiday represented. Most of us didn't care what it meant, other than eating great food and, more importantly, drinking margaritas, but we all thought it was to commemorate Mexico's Independence Day, a victory over Spain.

Marty, the Human Resources manager in our group, corrected that it was to celebrate Mexico's victory of a French occupation and that our mistake was yet another example of false memories of a group referred to as the Mandela Effect, named so after people who'd had an incorrect memory of Nelson Mandela dying in an African prison when he hadn't.

Marty shared other examples that seemed less significant: people remembered the name of Jif peanut butter as Jiffy; Curious George had a tail when he didn't; the theme song for Mister Rogers was "It's a beautiful day in the neighborhood" when it was "It's a beautiful day in *this* neighborhood"; and Hannibal Lecter said to Clarice Starling in *Silence of the Lambs* "Hello, Clarice" when, in fact, he simply said, "Good Morning."

"Get out," Frenchy said. "That movie scared the hell out of me."

"100% all true," Marty said. "It's even true individually. What people say in interviews about their own experience in previous jobs seems to be false memories compared to the reports from their supervisors when we check."

"You're kidding," Jan commented. "How do you know the former supervisors are telling you the truth?"

"We don't, but we have to somehow find middle ground," Marty said. "I have come to wonder what reality is."

"Well, the reality is these are the best damned margaritas I've ever had," Frenchy said, and everyone laughed.

"Except for the ones you had last week that you don't recall because you had too many," Jan said.

Agitator

My repairman didn't sit on his fat ass like the one in the commercial. He put in a new agitator in the washer last week, I had him coming back to install a third ice maker in my refrigerator, if he got the parts, and if he finished that project, I'd get him to change the lock on the front door, since it broke in the locked position.

If I got a package delivered, I'd have to go through the garage and walk around front, but I didn't mind, since that's about all the walking exercise I got with my cane after the doctor shaved the bone on my hammer toe that was agitated from rubbing up against the sole of my shoes. I didn't know much about toe pain until post-surgery.

The doctor really hadn't bothered sharing with me how long it would take for improvement. I think he was more concerned with milking my insurance to pay for that new sports car he looked ridiculous driving with the top down. He ought to befriend a dermatologist with that sunburn on his bald spot.

I could ride my stationary bicycle in the closet without much pain if I used the soles and heels of my feet to push the pedals, but the wheel inside the plastic covering had so much dust that it aggravated my allergies, and there was no way to clean that dust without disassembling.

When the repairman arrived, he wished me a Happy New Year, and I told him I'd seen better. He told me he understood and that this supply chain problem was wreaking havoc on everyone. People had been waiting on parts for months from stoves to cars, the big boys didn't care about repairs as long as the sales kept coming, which was where they made their money (In fact, there was speculation the supply chain problem was created to drive sales), and I told him that I blamed the government, both sides.

On the one hand, we had Biden who didn't know if he was coming or going any more than old horse-riding Ronald Reagan had, and on the other hand, the House seemed to waste time voting on a leader. I told him I knew how many licks it took to get to the center of a Tootsie roll pop more than I knew how many votes it took to elect a majority leader, and the government needed to stop spending borrowed money from China and take off their cufflinks, roll up their starched shirt sleeves, and get to the work of helping the people who sent them there instead of helping themselves.

He nodded, the toothpick bobbing up and down between his lips, and told me we were in the end times, the aliens would be back, and he felt like those aliens had planned the whole damned thing. He said we weren't any better than cats and dogs. We just think we're in charge.

I figured the pharmacy had run out of his meds since there had been that pharmaceutical problem with production in India, since the tampering incident, and I hobbled back to the den where I found I'd been locked out of Facebook and had somehow uploaded a business version that I couldn't figure out. I almost asked the repairman if he knew how to get in, but aside from the extra charges, I figured he'd think I was recording him or something. I entered shut down mode, turned on the television, and watched a rerun of an Andy Griffith show, the one where Earnest T. Bass is breaking windows, and I thought old Earnest T. might may have been the smartest character of all.

Garden Party

We went to a garden party. It was a birthday celebration for Stella who my wife knew socially from the garden club and who'd turned seventy-five. Stella had hired a band, a caterer, and a bartender, and the event took place in her canopied backyard with old growth oaks, magnolias, and ginkgo. The bartender served Bloody Marys with a splash of Worcestershire sauce to compliment the tomato juice and vodka and garnished the drink with a stalk of celery. Some sipped iced water with mint leaves. The tables were all draped in sage green plastic cloths, and each table had a round vase with hosta leaves covering the inside glass and a couple of white hydrangeas capping the vase. Of the forty or so guests, many of Stella's friends wore floral prints on linen or seersucker and sandals, and their husbands mostly wore khakis or shorts, loafers, a seasonal short sleeved shirt, and a few wore Panama hats.

Stella's husband Bill had dementia but was sociable and a great conversationalist though we'd heard he'd lost his filters. Most simply ignored him, and while he remembered my name, he didn't remember my wife's, told her she had pretty hair, but her feet were ugly. She'd just had a manicure and pedicure the day before, and on the way home, she looked at her feet and asked if I thought her feet were ugly. I rolled my eyes and simply said no and wondered if I got dementia if I might be honest about her ugly feet.

I told Bill it was a nice party he'd thrown for Stella, and he responded, "I didn't know anything about it." It was probably true. Stella had paid for it herself and arranged all the details. The garden party was a manifestation of her belief that she had to please herself first and foremost. She couldn't rely on her husband, anyone else, or even God. The woman was a steam roller in the community, she had a one-track mind, and if someone got in her way, he'd find himself as flat as Wile E. Coyote, hearing "Beep, beep" and watching Stella the Road Runner speed away.

Once we were seated, we made casual conversation with others while we listened to the Rat Pack-type trio sing mostly top Sinatra songs ("That's Life", "Fly Me to the Moon", "Something Stupid", "You Make Me Feel So Young", among others) from the elevated back porch. When the band took a break, a retired Methodist minister slurred a brief prayer, missed a step, and fell into one of the plucked hydrangeas while a couple rushed to help steady him. He waved off assistance but had a waddling gait to his car after the party.

The guests lined up for a feast of sliced ham, biscuits, candied bacon, veggies, fruit, pimento and cheese, and petit fours decorated like birthday cake. Stella spoke briefly, thanked friends, relatives, college buddies, and former work colleagues for coming. While gifts hadn't been requested, a few brought them anyway, but most had piled up cards on a table. The band and trio picked up with "My Way" while people nibbled, snacked, and knocked back Bloody Marys, some of which had more vodka than tomato juice.

Bill spilled his Bloody Mary, and it rushed like a tsunami onto Loretta's linen blouse, and he took napkins and rubbed them on her.

"That's okay, Bill. I've got it," Loretta said, and he responded, "Everybody sees that you've got some new ones," and continued to press her chest.

"Bill, that's enough," she snapped, and it was as though someone turned on a light and he became aware, wobbled back, stepped on a tree root, and fell sideways into two guests, hitting his head on the corner of the table on his way to the ground, where he was unconscious and bled slowly from the cut above his eye. If he could smell, he would have smelled dirt again like he had on the playground when he fell from the monkey bars in elementary school, when he hoed his mother's garden as a teen for hours, or when he dated a young Stella and they went to the stock car races on Friday nights, and the race cars sent clouds of dust from the dirt track into the stands.

Someone yelled "Stella!" and someone else yelled, "Call 911!"

Soon an ambulance arrived. Three EMTs placed Bill on a stretcher and loaded him in. Stella climbed into her car and followed them down the driveway and out of sight.

The garden party continued without Stella and Bill until the bartender was out of vodka, nothing remained on the serving dishes except crumbs, and the music stopped. One by one, the party goers slinked to their cars.

Thirst

The homeless man stood on the corner just up from the Santa Monica Pier by the triple water fountain that rested atop a column decorated with sea blue tile. He smiled, showing a set of mostly white teeth. He only wore tattered shorts, and the bottoms of his feet were filthy and revealed uncared for sores. His hair was unkempt and had formed dreadlocks that fell below his ears. He had a small paper cup in his right hand, filled it from one of the fountains, and then tossed the water onto different pavement squares on the sidewalk. We were in the souvenir store in search of magnets, coffee cups, and nice t-shirts, and while they shopped, I watched him from the store front window and could hear him through the opened doors.

"Okay?" he asked toward the sidewalk.

I wasn't sure to what he referred.

"I've got some blunts. You want one?" he asked a man coming out of the store, but the man ignored him.

I learned from the security guard near the door that the homeless man went by Gabe and lived in a tent just down from Santa Monica on Venice Beach. He combed the sands daily in search of treasures on his pilgrimage from Venice Beach to the Santa Monica Pier and back. He had a high school diploma, had gone to the community college, but dropped out when he couldn't pay back the loans. His already elderly parents couldn't help him, and when his mother died, and his father lost the house, they both camped in an abandoned Winnebago on the road's shoulder until they were herded to Skid Row in Los Angeles, an already sprawling fifty-city block homeless camp that had been there for ninety years since the 1930s. The guard explained that finally a tough love judge had called for audits of charities and government entities and ordered a fund established to house and care for the homeless once and for all.

Gabe and his father had headed to Venice Beach, but his father fell into the cactus garden in Beverly Hills, got an infection, and died. Gabe ended up following a tarot card reader to Venice Beach shortly after, and together they scooped enough coins and bills in their hat from her readings and his dancing to outdated music to buy enough food to survive day to day. She'd told him she was going to Malibu one day, and he never saw her again. What little he'd made from panhandling, he bought food and legal marijuana and stayed high most of the time.

"What's he doing with the water?"

"He's feeding the gremlins."

"What?"

"He thinks there are gremlins following him around, and they are thirsty."

"Gremlins like the ones in the movies?"

"Yeah. They were the manufactured Hollywood creatures in the movies. He's tossing the water for them to lick off the pavement. The water evaporates, and it reinforces that they are lapping it up."

"That's nuts."

"Well, to him, it's real. I suspect he's smoked some stuff that probably sent him even further over the edge. He's harmless though. I can't give him a lot, but occasionally, I give him a few bucks."

It seemed to me that like most Americans, I was one paycheck away from being like Gabe, and because I wasn't like Gabe, I needed to help in some small way. I walked outside.

"Hey, Gabe."

He turned toward me but continued to fill the cup and toss water on the pavement. I handed him a fifty-dollar bill, and he put it in his pocket and continued to help his gremlins quench their thirst. The fifty probably wouldn't help him much, or even for long, but I walked away feeling like it was the right thing to do.

Little Dom's

Christina and I got engaged at Griffith Observatory overlooking Los Angeles at sunset. We had done most pre-marriage necessities—met each other's dysfunctional families, shared about previous relationships, and agreed on future goals. We paid the fee to park, walked to the edge of the cliff nearest the Hollywood sign, and stood breathing in the view of the sprawling city below. We saw a light zoom across the sky, a UFO we assumed, and which underscored the importance of the moment. I bent down on one knee, pulled the engagement ring from my pocket, and asked her, "Will you marry me?"

"Yes," she said, tearing up.

I stood to applause. There were visitors and park officials who had watched the proposal. It made the moment even more special. After talking about moving in together, what we might keep of mine, how the commute might work for my job downtown, we got into my Jeep and headed back down the mountain to Little Dom's, an Italian restaurant where I'd made reservations. Though I felt like she might say "Yes" I honestly didn't know and figured if she said "No" then we might keep the dinner reservations, talk through the "No" or simply skip dinner, making someone else on the waiting list a happy diner.

We had the appetizer rice balls, the vegan spaghetti entre, and indulged in a delicious olive oil cake with a strawberry-rhubarb topping. We asked a Canadian couple at the next table to take our photo, and then I excused myself. In the restroom, I noticed a person who seemed familiar washing his hands. We both nodded. He wore a cap, a plaid short sleeved shirt, jeans, and Vans. Back at our table, I saw him at a nearby booth with his date, a petite brunette with haunting eyes who also looked familiar. She wore a comfortable linen dress and sandals.

"Christina, do you see the couple two booths from our table to your left, my right?"

"Yes, I do. I noticed them come in. I may be wrong, but I think that's Megan Fox. She played in the *Transformers* movies."

"Oh yeah. What about her date?"

"I think that's Machine Gun Kelly. See the tattoos on his arms, the white hair hanging out from under that hat?"

"Yeah. I saw him in the restroom. He looked familiar."

"I think it's cool we can go to a neighborhood restaurant like Little Dom's and see stars."

"Especially since we are so close to the observatory. You want to get their autographs?"

"No, let them eat in peace. That's what makes this place special. It's not all paparazzi."

I stood with my phone, turned on the flash, and took photos at different angles. I moved around, Christina threw back her head, pushed out her arm, dangled her left hand with the engagement ring I'd financed, and people clapped, even Megan Fox and Machine Gun Kelly. As we waltzed out of the restaurant, I said, "I'll always be your paparazzi."

Engagement Ring

After I asked my girlfriend to marry me and she said yes, I needed to get a ring. I didn't have the funds to purchase one without plunging into debt, and like my dad who collected used pizza pans to give away for wedding gifts, my aunt who recycled roadkill into art, and my grandmother who reused paper plates, cups, and tin foil, I had been conditioned to be frugal, look for deals, and scan trash piles for treasures.

I wondered if my aunts who'd had multiple marriages had kept their engagement rings. I called them, asked to borrow them, and they all said, "Hope it'll bring you more luck than it did me." I told them I'd give them some money once my girlfriend made a choice.

I unzipped the freezer bag and spread the treasures on the kitchen table. My girlfriend smiled, told me she appreciated my creativity, but she wanted her own ring, not a ring from one of my aunts' failed marriages. I understood her logic, appreciated her recognition of my frugality, and after taking out a high interest loan, I bought her a small quarter carat diamond set in yellow gold.

I did not, however, tell her the flowers I wooed her with for months before our engagement had been ones I plucked from fresh arrangements placed on new graves in the cemetery. I knew the carnations, roses, and lilies would bring her more joy than the recently planted.

How to Spend Christmas Alone at Motel 6

I bought a brown mink shawl as a Christmas present for my wife. I found it in second-hand store for ninety dollars. The lady at the counter gave me ten percent off because it hadn't sold in three years, and she was glad to be rid of it. Said there'd been times she forgot it was there, turned on the lights, and thought it was a wild animal that had gotten in the store.

The shawl had the name *Emily Chesterfield* sewn onto the tag, and when I asked some local friends, they shared she'd been the wife of a merchant who owned a store downtown before the mall in the suburbs lured shoppers away. The store had closed and fallen into a state of disrepair after the Chesterfields passed away. The old building had been rented a few times: a dollar store, a tattoo parlor, and title and loan business.

I figured it would be hilarious if I found Emily's grave and took a photo to place in the gift-wrapped box. I went out at lunch and got a good shot of the granite head stone and showed it to my friends, but they cautioned me that my sense of humor was morbid and that my wife might not find it humorous at all.

She was excited when she ripped into the candy cane wrapping paper, tore off the bow, cut the tape with her fingernails. When she opened the box, she "oohed" and "aahed" about the mink until she saw the name stitched into the tag and saw the head stone photo. "What the hell?"

I laughed, told her Merry Christmas.

She threw the box and mink at me and stormed out of the living room boo-hooing.

"It was a joke," I told her. "I thought you'd like the mink."

"It's not funny. Get the hell out of here," she said.

"What about our eggnog?"

"Take it to the cemetery and drink it with Emily," she said. "I've had it."

It was sad that the clerk at Motel 6 remembered my name from the last time. I hoped my wife would simmer down and take me back in a few days.

Polo Shirts

My friend Tom showed up at school wearing a nice Polo shirt with the polo player emblem stitched on the left breast. We "oohed" and "aahed" and didn't understand how his mother was able to afford it on her cookie factory pay, but at lunch when I traded him my bologna sandwich for his Little Debbie cream pie, he shared the truth: his mom bought the inexpensive Polo socks, cut the polo emblem off, and sewed them onto plain, no brand shirts. He would be in style and not look so poor. He even told me to look at the label on the inside of the shirt on his neck for proof.

When Tom didn't show for our twenty-fifth high school reunion, I called him. He shared he didn't have the money to travel because he'd cashed out equity from his house for the third time to get his wife a new car. She was embarrassed to drive the old Vega. I asked him about his mortgage, and he shared he had a six percent interest rate over thirty years. We promised to visit, and when I got off the phone, I figured by the time he paid the interest, paid the refinance fees, and added all the equity he cashed out, the hundred-and-fifty-thousand-dollar mortgage will have cost him over a million dollars.

Panhandler

The bearded panhandler stood by the stop sign at the corner of Hollywood and the off ramp to the hospital from 6:30 a.m. until after rush hour in the afternoon. He held a cardboard sign that read *Hungry. Please help.* He collected wads of ones, fives, and occasionally, a ten, twenty, or even a sausage biscuit from employees of the hospital who were ethically bound to help. He had a stack of empty water bottles littered on the grass for city employees to clean up and tied his one-eyed dog to a light pole. I felt like there were plenty of jobs in town for him since COVID but not tax-free ones. One night, I left work later than usual, drove down Hollywood, saw him getting into a new SUV in a nearby parking lot, and followed him to a curbside pickup at the Outback Steakhouse. I videoed him on my phone and emailed my discovery to the evening news channel. I saw him two weeks later near a Wal-Mart entrance, sporting a baseball cap, a clean-shaven face, and panhandling with a new cardboard sign that read *Lost job. Need Help* and decided that while I might give him credit for persistence and creativity, I still wouldn't hand over my hard-earned money to the panhandler.

Made in the USA
Columbia, SC
31 March 2024